BLACK
TUESDAY

BLACK

TUESDAY

SUSAN COLEBANK

DUTTON CHILDREN'S BOOKS

DUTTON CHILDREN'S BOOKS
A division of Penguin Young Readers Group

Published by the Penguin Group
Penguin Group (USA) Inc., 375 Hudson Street, New York, New York 10014, U.S.A. ● Penguin Group (Canada), 90 Eglinton Avenue East, Suite 700, Toronto, Ontario, Canada M4P 2Y3 (a division of Pearson Penguin Canada Inc.) ● Penguin Books Ltd, 80 Strand, London WC2R 0RL, England ● Penguin Ireland, 25 St Stephen's Green, Dublin 2, Ireland (a division of Penguin Books Ltd) ● Penguin Group (Australia), 250 Camberwell Road, Camberwell, Victoria 3124, Australia (a division of Pearson Australia Group Pty Ltd) ● Penguin Books India Pvt Ltd, 11 Community Centre, Panchsheel Park, New Delhi - 110 017, India ● Penguin Group (NZ), 67 Apollo Drive, Rosedale, North Shore 0745, Auckland, New Zealand (a division of Pearson New Zealand Ltd) ● Penguin Books (South Africa) (Pty) Ltd, 24 Sturdee Avenue, Rosebank, Johannesburg 2196, South Africa ● Penguin Books Ltd, Registered Offices: 80 Strand, London WC2R 0RL, England

Library of Congress Cataloging-in-Publication Data
Colebank, Susan.
Black Tuesday / by Susan Colebank. — 1st ed.
p. cm.
Summary: An over-achieving Phoenix high school student's life changes dramatically when she is responsible for a car crash that kills a child, and she goes from honors classes and tennis team captain to doing community service and rebelling against her controlling mother.
[1. Traffic accidents—Fiction. 2. High schools—Fiction. 3. Schools—Fiction. 4. Interpersonal relations—Fiction. 5. Family life—Arizona—Fiction. 6. Arizona—Fiction.] I. Title.
PZ7.C67363Bl 2007
[Fic]—dc22 2006031792

Published in the United States by Dutton Children's Books,
a member of Penguin Young Readers Group
345 Hudson Street, New York, New York 10014
www.penguin.com/youngreaders

Designed by Irene Vandervoort

Printed in USA First Edition
ISBN 978-0-525-47766-2
10 9 8 7 6 5 4 3 2 1

For Jason,
who believes in my dreams

BLACK
TUESDAY

1

GET OFF OF HER!"

Jayne Thompkins felt one of those heart palpitations her grams was always talking about. Her barely teenage sister was under a boy.

A boy who had his hand on the side of her sister's breast.

And her sister was just lying there, taking it like a future pregnant fourteen-year-old.

Jayne closed her eyes for a second, willing this to all go away so she could get out of here and still make it to tennis on time. Which would be good, considering she'd just been made captain. Being on time seemed like a captainlike thing to do.

She took a slow, measured breath. Jayne thought back to her psychology class last semester, to the section that had talked about stress. Stress was a perception. She could choose to be stressed or not.

She opened her eyes. This guy's hand was still squeezing her sister's flesh. Or might as well have been. The Victoria's Secret bra wasn't exactly a deterrent. Not with Ellie's T-shirt bunched up at the head of the bed.

Yep, Jayne felt stressed all right.

The boy with the tanned, shirtless back barely looked up at her. He either hadn't noticed her or he was having too much fun licking Ellie's collarbone in rhythm to the booty call music blaring around them.

Jayne snapped off the CD player and turned back to her sister. That boy hadn't moved an inch.

Then again, neither had Ellie. *Ellie, you're a freakin' idiot. About boys. About grades. About taking your insulin shot.*

About life in general.

Ellie should've been watching bad Hilary Duff movies, not letting her boobies get felt up by this schmuck. Jayne was used to her sister's flavor-of-the-week infatuations. But the boobie action going on here? Jayne hadn't even experienced that yet at the ripe old age of sixteen.

And if *she* wasn't ready for third base, Ellie sure wasn't.

Ellie finally opened her eyes and saw Jayne standing there. Frantically, she pushed at the oblivious ball of hormones panting on top of her. "Danny, get up."

The guy's lips started working their way down Ellie's chest. "Why?" He laughed as he said the word. "It's just your sister."

Jayne's blood temperature rose a few degrees. This Abercrombie & Fitch reject didn't seem to appreciate the situation he was in.

"That's right. I'm just her sister." Jayne gripped his waistband, using the weight of her body to get his private bits off of Ellie's. "But if you don't want to find out firsthand where our mother stashed the bodies of all the other Neanderthals who tried to get statutory with my sister, you better get up."

Danny was barely upright when Jayne started pushing him, barefoot and shirtless, toward the bedroom door. "Out," she demanded.

Jayne turned to see Ellie reach blindly behind her and grab her own shirt, pulling it over the C-cups she'd gotten over the past year.

Ellie'd gone from looking scared at being caught with a boy in her room to pissed off. "Does Mom have you spying on me now?"

Jayne stopped mid-push. Yeah, in between studying thirty hours a week and spending what felt like every non-sleeping minute building up her college résumé, she was spying on Ellie for the fun of it. "Don't be a jerk. I forgot my tennis shoes this morning and was just heading upstairs to get them. But then I heard a bunch of giggling in here, Chuckles."

A blush tinged Ellie's cheeks. "Oh."

Jayne found herself leaning her full weight against Danny, but he had come to a standstill. "I'm not going out there like this," he said, pointing at his bare chest, his tiny pubescent nipples the size of peas.

Jayne looked at the Hello Kitty clock on Ellie's dresser. Jayne was a practical girl, if nothing else. She was also a girl who knew the value of deadlines. "You have one minute to find everything you brought with you or else it goes into the next Thompkins garage sale."

Danny started picking up his discarded clothes. Progress, finally. But he stopped when he saw Jayne following two steps behind him. "Do you mind? I can dress myself."

"That remains to be seen." She forced herself to stand still.

Stalking the half-naked guy definitely wasn't going to get him to move faster.

She lifted the flap of her messenger bag she'd come in with and pulled out a folder. "When I was at the career center today, I saw something you might be interested in."

Ellie crossed her arms, creating two inches of cleavage. "I already told you, I'm not going to college. I'm not some sheep that—"

"—that needs to follow the herd. So you've told me a bajillion times. But this is different." Jayne sat down next to Ellie, opened the folder, and dropped a stapled packet in her sister's lap. "The Fashion Institute of Technology's having a contest open to sophomores, juniors, and seniors."

Ellie shrugged. But she started flipping through the pages. "I don't need a stinking fashion college in order to break into fashion. Gianni Versace didn't go to one. Coco Chanel didn't either."

"But Calvin Klein went to FIT."

Ellie made a farting sound with her mouth. "He's totally commercial. And uninspired."

"Michael Kors did, too. I've heard you say you think he's genius."

Again, Jayne felt Ellie's shoulders move. But her sister kept turning the pages, which was a good sign. Anything that made Ellie think about a life that extended beyond boys, the mall, and the next party was a good thing.

The bathroom door shut. Ellie's make-out boy had just gone behind it.

Jayne felt her head wrinkle up. She called out, "You better pee fast, pretty boy. I don't have all day."

Normally, Jayne didn't like confrontations. But then again, these last few minutes hadn't been too normal. She started jiggling her leg. If their mom caught this guy here . . . But why would she? She was at the studio, getting ready for the six o'clock news.

"Anyway, the ten-thousand-dollar prize money FIT is offering is free and clear." Jayne tightened her ponytail, her leg still going at it like jackhammer. Once she got that guy out of here, she might actually make it to tennis on time. "You don't have to get a degree at their school or anything. You just have to design a twenty-piece collection, sew up one outfit, and turn in everything by August first."

"That's four months from now." Ellie's voice rose a couple of octaves, but her eyes were bright. Jayne knew she'd hooked her.

"Elle, I've been wearing your stuff since you made your first cut-up, tie-dyed, hand-painted T-shirt at age eight. You totally have a chance."

Ellie looked at Jayne, the pissiness gone from her clear blue eyes. Eyes she'd gotten from their dad, while Jayne had gotten the boring hazel-green eyes their mom had. As with everything in life, Ellie had managed to come out on top even in the genes department.

Sure, Jayne Lee Thompkins had made out in the brains department. But it might've been fun to be the cute, irresponsible one for once.

Jayne crossed her arms, her hands encircling the hard biceps she'd built up over the last ten years of tennis clinics. She leaned against Ellie and teased, "Then again, if I'd known you were getting felt up today, I would've left school earlier and headed over to Walgreens to buy you a box of Trojans."

"Awesome." Danny stood at the bathroom door, his backpack slung over a shoulder. His shirt and shoes were on, and he was tucking his blond hair behind his ears. The ends flipped out like a girl's bob.

"I was joking, jerkwad." After a quick glare in the guy's direction, she turned back to Ellie and the packet of papers she was still flipping through. "Just think about it, okay? You win the contest, you get the money, *and* you get to go to FIT for six weeks next summer. In New York. Where all your idols live." Jayne waved a hand around the room at the fashion ads Ellie had been tearing out of *Vogue* and *Bazaar* for the last six years.

Ellie snorted. "You mean *if*."

"No. I mean *when*," Jayne said with a smile.

Suddenly, the front door slammed shut. "Ellie? Jayne? You girls home?"

Ellie stared wide-eyed and slack-jawed at Jayne.

Their mom was home.

Ellie was screwed.

2

CRAP!" Ellie said. "She's going to kill me."

Jayne cleared her head, like she did right before she took a test. In order to outsmart her mom, she had to treat this whole situation like a test. "We'll just say the jerkwad here was helping you study, Elle. Don't worry about it."

"Don't worry about it?" Ellie bit down on one of her cotton-candy-pink nails. "Jaynie, Mom grounded me this week because I'm getting a D in pre-algebra. I'm not supposed to have anyone over."

"We'll just say Dennis here was tutoring you in pre-algebra."

"Yo, it's Danny."

Jayne hissed, "Keep your voice down, idiot."

"But that won't work. Mom paid for a tutor." Ellie looked like a beaver with a log, the way she was going at her nail.

"We'll just say Danny here's that tutor."

"Uh-uh. Won't work. Mom made sure they gave me a girl because of my 'boy-crazy tendencies.'"

Jayne exhaled. She shouldn't be this tense. After all, it wasn't like her mom was the Antichrist. Then again, Ellie always liked to say she didn't have the fear of God in her—just the fear of Gen Thompkins.

"What are we going to do?" Ellie whispered, her words coming out like a mouse on helium.

They both knew that boys weren't allowed at the Thompkins homestead when no parent was around. And boys were definitely never allowed in either of their bedrooms, the only exceptions being paramedics and firemen if one of them was dying. As in not breathing.

Bleeding and unconscious didn't count.

Evasive action was needed. Now. Jayne called out, "We're in Ellie's room, Mom. We'll be right there!"

"Whose car is that in the driveway?" Jayne should've known their mom wasn't going to back off that easily.

Jayne racked her brain for a good explanation. Just like during a test, she mulled her options. None were good. And just like during a test, she opted to skip this question for later. "Mom, can't hear you! We'll be out in a minute!"

She turned to the boy in her sister's room. Judging by the look of terror on his face, he definitely didn't want to face Gen Thompkins. She was the kind of woman who convinced fathers to send their sons to military schools. Word on the street was she'd already done it twice.

Only Jayne and Ellie knew the truth. And how close the rumor was to the truth. Gen had powerful friends. That didn't bode well for the boys who messed with her daughters.

"Okay, we need a plan," Jayne said, looking around the pale rose room. Her eyes stopped on the door leading to the adjoining bathroom. "The bathroom window. Let's go."

Danny and Ellie ran ahead of her into bathroom and then stopped. "That window's like five feet up!" Danny whined.

"Keep your voice down!" Jayne surveyed the window and the claw-foot tub under it. "Ellie, bring your desk chair in here."

Jayne grabbed the chair her sister dragged in and positioned it under the window. She went up first, sliding the window open before pushing the screen out with the palms of her hands. "Okay, listen, David, Denny, dipwad." She climbed off the chair. "Whatever your name is. Your skinny butt should fit through here. There's a natal plum bush below it, so your fall should be cushioned."

"Fall?" A lock of girly hair fell over his eye.

Jayne arched an eyebrow at him. "Military school?"

He scowled at her and stepped onto the chair.

"Wait." She stopped him from climbing through the window by hooking a finger through his belt loop. "Make sure you put the screen between the bush and the house to hide it. I'll pop it back in later."

He started to pull himself through the window. Jayne yanked him back down again.

"What!"

"You're going to have to leave your car here."

"Whatever." His scowl told her he thought she was nuts. And that she could go to hell.

"Do you want my mother seeing you drive away?"

"No, but I don't really want to walk ten miles to get home."

Jayne had to admit that it was pretty hot for April. Then again, Paradise Valley, a suburb of Phoenix, was usually pushing the triple digits this time of year, and this big whiny baby should be used to it. She said in a low, rushed voice, "You should have thought of that before introducing yourself to my sister's boobies."

Jayne pushed him through the window and closed it.

"Girls?" The three of them stopped talking as the bedroom door handle jiggled. "Everything okay in there?"

Jayne's mind raced to think of an excuse. What could buy them time with Gen Thompkins, the mother who micromanaged every minute of their lives when she wasn't micromanaging her career?

"We're putting highlights in Ellie's hair, Mom. I'm on a roll with the foil, or else I'd get the door." Jayne's mind raced, trying to cover any loophole she hadn't thought about. "Gustav couldn't fit us in, so we got our own kit."

"I've warned you girls about those box highlights. I hope you're not turning that gorgeous hair of Ellie's orange."

It was just like her mom to think Jayne was screwing up. Jayne had never gotten anything less than an A-minus in her entire life, but her mom still found a way to harp about a minus.

Her mom's voice pierced through the door again, breaking through Jayne's thoughts. "Whose car is that out front?"

Back to that question again. Jayne wasn't fooled by the no-nonsense, sane tone of her mom's newscaster voice. She knew that if any of them played this the wrong way, her mom would get a drill and pry the door off its hinges.

Ellie looked at Jayne, speechless again. When it came to standing up to their mom, Ellie had a way of becoming a big useless blob.

Which usually turned Jayne into a big fat liar. All for the sake of saving Ellie's butt. "One of Ellie's friends took her to get the highlights, and when they got here, the girl ran out of gas. Dan . . . ielle took the bus."

Jayne winced. Even she thought the story was Swiss cheese.

"You couldn't have just given her a ride?"

"The bus stop is just outside, Mom. The girl had some appointment she had to get to, and I'm trying to finish up Ellie's hair before tennis practice."

Jayne had already figured out this fictitious girl was going to decide that she didn't have time to come back here tonight to pick up her car. That meant Jayne had to deal with the car later.

Jayne held her breath. She wasn't the greatest at lying, but the key was to play the scenario out like a little movie in her head. That's how she figured out tests: she put herself back at her desk in her room, with her CDs playing in the background, and she tried to remember during what part of which song she'd memorized the bit of information that she had momentarily forgotten.

She knew her mom's next questions before she asked them.

"Who is Danielle?"

"She's one of Ellie's mall posse."

"And why aren't you at tennis practice yet? Doesn't it start at four?"

"Practice starts late today. Coach had a teachers' meeting." Jayne grimaced at Ellie. Her stomach hurt. Lying had a weird way of doing that to her.

The girls were quiet as they waited to see Gen's reaction.

Ellie whispered, "Danielle? Mom's going to want to meet her

at some point. Nice, Jayne. Couldn't you have used one of my real friends?"

"You have a car out there that doesn't belong to either Janice or Megan, dweeb." Jayne checked her watch. For once, she wanted time to move faster. "And you better remember all this when Mom quizzes you later. I didn't put my butt on the line so you could screw me over."

They heard their mom's heels click down the hall. "Well, make sure you get out of here in the next ten minutes so you're not late, Jayne. Harvard's not going to take you just on grades alone."

Jayne wanted to say, *Well, duh*. She wanted to so badly. The words were there, on the tip of her tongue. She just had to open her mouth and say them.

But she didn't. Instead, like usual, she sucked the words down.

3

C'MON, THOMPKINS. What's the answer to twenty-three?"

Jayne hunkered over her paper. She had two more essay questions to go and fifteen minutes left. She didn't have time for Lori Parnell.

Instead, she needed to spend the next nine hundred seconds worrying about herself.

Jayne took another look at the clock. Fourteen minutes and counting. Her eyes hurriedly scanned the question again, her leg jiggling. *If F. Scott Fitzgerald were alive today, would he have written* Gatsby . . .

"You suck, Thompkins."

Jayne sat up a little straighter. Lori was a jerk. But she should've been used to the Loris of the world. She'd been dealing with them since first grade, when she won her first class spelling bee and someone called her a poophead.

She put Lori out of her mind. Or tried. She looked at the clock. Twelve minutes left.

C'mon, Jayne. You know you don't suck. What is going to suck is you flunking this test because you didn't finish these two essay questions. And then blowing an A average. Harvard won't like that much. And your mom definitely won't like that.

She ended up finishing the essay questions right before the bell rang. But she wasn't happy with her answers.

Or the way she had let Lori harass her.

"You're sure I'm still number one?"

"Yes, Jayne." Angie Challen, junior guidance counselor and all-around granola, folded her hands on top of the file in front of her. She had tiny bird hands that went with the messy nest of red hair secured on top of her head with three number-two pencils.

She didn't look too upset with Jayne's line of questioning. After all, Jayne'd been asking the same question for the last two and a half years.

Miss Challen was also a family friend and knew how much Jayne and her parents wanted Jayne to get into a good school. And by *parents* she meant *Jayne's mother*. And by *good school* she meant *Harvard*. She knew Jayne's dad would be happy to see her go to college—any college.

But Gen Thompkins liked to say, "The rest are crap, Jayne. And I'm not sending my daughter to a crap school like I had to go to."

Miss Challen winked at Jayne. "If you want, you can stand over my shoulder while I add everything together again."

Jayne pushed herself away from the doorjamb. "That's okay, I believe you."

She smoothed her blue tennis skirt over her thighs. She had the highest GPA for the eleventh quarter in a row. She only had to keep it up for five more quarters—then she'd be valedictorian.

And then she'd be off for four more years of straight A's.

Crap.

Where'd that come from? That . . . resignation? Sure, she had to work for A's. She sometimes had to put in forty hours of studying a week.

She liked studying. She liked A's. No big deal.

But sometimes it'd be nice to be normal, like . . . going to the mall. And slurping an Orange Julius with Ellie. And not getting an "I told you so" look from her mom when she got an A-minus a few days later.

She stole a glance at her watch. Twenty-five minutes to get to practice. Between meeting with Janice to talk about the car wash for the French Club next week and now sharing small talk with Miss Challen, she was running late. She had to be on time today. After covering for Ellie yesterday, she knew that if she was late today, Coach could quite possibly make Missy Travers captain.

And Missy Travers didn't deserve captain. She always hit her forehands into the net. Missy getting to put "captain" on *her* college résumé was totally unacceptable.

"Did you turn in the Senior Student application?"

"Yesterday." The Senior Student was the best academic award in Phoenix. Probably even in Arizona. The winner got to spend all four summers during college living and learning in different places around the world. Like excavating in Egypt and learning about wildlife preservation in Alaska.

Over one thousand people were said to apply for it.

Jayne didn't care where the scholarship took her, as long as it was far away from her insane family.

"Sent in my transcripts, my three letters of recommendation, and an essay about my greatest personal achievement."

"Which was?"

"My grades."

Miss Challen looked up at the ceiling and shook her head. "Grades aren't an achievement, Jayne. They're more of a quantifier for the achievements you make in each class."

"Exactly. And I've accumulated a lot of great quantifiers."

Jayne had actually written about a different topic. About how hard it was to stay motivated through almost all twelve years of school and still get A's a hundred percent of the time.

But that was too personal to share with Miss Challen. She hadn't shared it with anyone, actually.

"Hey, before I get going, what number is Tom? Tom Gerome?" Jayne couldn't help herself. Tom may have been her best friend, but he was also her closest academic competitor.

"He has the second-highest grade in the junior class."

"By how much?"

Miss Challen shook her head and tsked, but she kept smiling. Jayne knew that smile. The academic adviser had always told Jayne she was the most competitive, grade-focused person she'd ever met in her life. "You know I can't divulge that information."

Jayne shrugged, splitting her blonde ponytail apart and pulling it tighter. "That's okay." She grinned. "I'll ask the loser later."

"Always good to see what a good sport you are, Jayne."

Jayne said the words she always heard her mother say, but she said them with the humor her mother always lacked: "It's called having a healthy competitive spirit."

Jayne was walking down the last hallway, heading toward the parking lot, when her cell phone rang. She checked the caller ID before flipping the phone open. "Sucked any face today?"

"Not yet," Ellie chirped back, "but the day's still young. Hey, are you still at school?"

"Yeah. I'm on my way to practice. I've got"—she checked her watch—"fifteen minutes to get over to the club. What's up?"

"I left my biology homework in my locker. Could you get it for me?"

Jayne slowed down her steps, but she didn't stop. "I'm really running late, Elle. And Coach Reynolds told me he'd make Missy captain if I was late again. She'll love gloating about that."

"She's just pissed that you're only a junior and she's a senior."

"Yeah, I guess." Jayne felt her feet slowing down even more, her body warring with her brain. Her brain knew she had to get to practice. Her heart—and her feet—knew that Ellie was flunking biology. FIT didn't care if prospective students had a 4.0 GPA, but it definitely wasn't looking for students with a D or F average.

Jayne turned and went back down the hall, walking fast and furious. Ellie wasn't the brain in this family. A bad science grade might have a domino effect on the rest of her grades and lead Ellie to drop out, get a GED, and live in a double-wide trailer out in Mesa. Bye-bye, bright future. "Fine. I'm on my way to pick up your homework, slacker."

"You know you're my favorite sister, right?"

Before Jayne could call Ellie on the load of crap she was shoveling her way, Lori Parnell and her best friend, Jenna Deavers, sprinted by in their blue-and-white cheerleading uniforms. They were two of the most popular girls at Palm Desert High, not because they were the smartest or the prettiest or even that nice, but because they were the meanest.

Behind their backs, everyone called them the Wicked Witches of the East and West.

But to their faces, everyone was nice. That was because they ran a blog that no one wanted to be on: *Palm Desert's Pathetic Losers.*

No one who was anyone wanted to make that list. As a result, everyone invited them to their parties. And kept the Wicked Witch comments to themselves.

Jayne hadn't made the list. What were they going to say about her? *Jayne's too smart and gets all A's. What a loser.* Ow. The pain.

As they trotted past her, Lori called out, "Does it ever get tiring to be such a wench?"

I don't know. How does it feel, lard butt?

In her head, she said the words. But Jayne didn't say them aloud. Even though she could've. Lori must've had the most cellulite of any sixteen-year-old, ever.

Jenna giggled. She was always giggling over anything Lori said. That's what lackeys usually did.

Jenna said, "Wench. Awesome word."

"Who are you talking to?" Ellie's voice pulled Jayne out of her thoughts about the Wicked Witches.

"No one important." Jayne stopped at her sister's locker. She tried to get Tweedledum and Tweedledumber out of her head. Otherwise, her backhand was going to be crap today. "What's your locker combo again?"

Ellie recited the numbers. "I totally owe you one, Jayne."

"Yeah?" She started turning the dial. "What are you going to do for me if Missy gets made captain?"

"I'll make like Tonya Harding and break her kneecap."

4

ONE BIOLOGY HOMEWORK assignment later, Jayne made her way to the underclassmen parking lot. It was behind the football field and as far as a person could walk and still stay on campus.

She had about twelve minutes to get to practice.

"Jayne!"

"What!" Jayne didn't even turn around. She knew that voice. She'd first heard it in fourth grade asking to borrow a pencil.

"Have you been to see Challen?" A boy with wavy brown hair and a runner's body loped up beside her.

"Do you even have to ask, Tommy?" Jayne spared him a sideways glance as she pulled out her car keys.

"Then you know you're number two?" He tried, but he just couldn't hold the lie. His left eye blinked. That left eye of his was Jayne's lie detector. No blink—he was telling the truth. Blink—he was lying.

"Nice try. I'm still holding at number one."

"Well, did you know *I'm* number two?" He jostled her with an elbow in the ribs. He smelled like Old Spice deodorant and

Bengay. He'd done a few too many curls the other day at the gym when he tried to out-curl Jayne. He'd forgotten to take into account that he had a thirty-five-pound dumbbell and she'd been using a ten-pounder.

"Yeah, I did." Jayne smiled up at him, squinting against the sun and into his dark blue eyes. Tom really had the nicest eyes she'd ever seen outside of Ellie's. "That makes Jenna Deavers number three."

Jenna was a witch, but she was a smart witch.

"Four."

"What?" Jayne was almost shocked enough to slow down her speed walk. "How?"

"A B-minus in PE."

Jayne smiled. She believed in karma, and Jenna had just gotten a visit. "That makes sense. She spent a month in study hall instead of PE because we had to run a hundred laps in four weeks. So she made up some inner ear thing to get out of it."

Jayne spotted her sweet-sixteen birthday present at the far end of the parking lot and pointed her remote at it. The white Jetta's headlights blinked and the horn beeped as she unlocked the doors.

Tom wiped at his mouth with the neck of his "Property of Palm Desert High" gym shirt. "Why are you still here? Don't you have tennis practice?"

"Ellie called and—"

"—and she asked for favor 3,298. Got it." Tom put a hand on her elbow to slow her down. "Hey, I heard about Danny Broden's car. Genius."

"Thanks." Jayne flashed him a smile before focusing again

on the car. One call to a tow-truck company had solved all of Jayne's problems. Ellie's little boy toy hadn't been too happy about his visit to Joe's Tow Service, but when Jayne reminded him about how cold the military schools got in Alaska, he'd shut up.

Tom cleared his throat and lightly touched her forearm. "I have to get to track practice, but I was wondering if I could talk to you for a second."

"Weren't we just doing that?" She had to get to practice herself. The panicked feeling in Jayne's stomach was starting to spread through her whole body.

She pulled away from his grasp and opened the car door, throwing her book bag on the passenger seat. "Give me a call later, 'kay? If I'm late, I can kiss being captain good-bye." She put on a pair of wire-rimmed sunglasses hanging from her visor. "And you know Missy's going to lord it over me the rest of the year if that happens."

They smiled at each other as they said in unison: "Bee-yotch."

Yep, Tom was her best friend for a reason. They definitely were on the same wavelength. Not on a boyfriend-girlfriend level, but that would've just messed things up anyway. Romantic feelings always messed things up.

Ellie was the prime example of that.

Jayne punched the key into the ignition and turned toward Tom. He looked like he was going to say more but changed his mind.

"I won't be home till late," he said, "so I'll talk to you tomorrow at school."

"Or e-mail me tonight."

"That's okay. It can wait until tomorrow."

Jayne didn't notice the tiny blush on Tom's face. She was already closing the door and thinking how fast she could drive to practice without getting pulled over.

The clock on the dashboard said 3:57. *Come on, come on, come on!* She was behind a grandma in a Toyota Camry whose left blinker had been on for the last five blocks. They were going twenty-eight in a thirty-five zone on a two-lane road. Jayne had half a mind to cross the double line and pass the clueless driver. The fear of getting pulled over by a hidden cop stopped her.

She really didn't have time to devote a Saturday to traffic school.

Beethoven's Fifth started playing over the CD that had started up as soon as she'd turned on the car. Jayne flipped open her cell, not even checking the caller ID. Ellie probably wanted to cajole her into doing her biology homework.

That was so not going to happen.

Again.

"What is it now?"

"Jayne! Good. I have two minutes before I meet with my producer and I need to talk to you."

Jayne clenched the steering wheel. Gen Thompkins was Arizona's number-one-rated newscaster. She reigned over the six o'clock and nine o'clock news on channel 16. The five-year-old show had Gen in her element: wearing thousand-dollar Saks Fifth Avenue suits while stirring up eggs Benedict with a local five-star chef or getting on-air Botox from the best plastic surgeon in the Sonoran Desert.

"What do you need to talk about?" Jayne's foot hovered over the brake while she silently cursed the mentally deficient driver in front of her.

"As usual, I'm up to my ears in work." As usual, her mom was in "me" mode. "But I really want to do something for your dad's forty-fifth." She paused. "I want us to throw your dad a surprise party."

The grandma in the Camry finally turned, making a right as the left-turn signal continued blinking. Jayne jammed her foot on the accelerator and tried to keep from looking at the clock.

She heard her mom mutter something to someone on her side of the line before turning her attention back to Jayne. Gen liked to think she could multitask, but she wasn't good at it. Something—or someone—always ended up getting the short end of the stick.

"Now, we both know you're on much better terms with your grandmother than I am," she started saying. "I need you to call your grandmother and have her bring some baby pictures of your father. I want to get the production guys here at the station to put together a slide show, a kind of *This Is Your Life* thing."

Jayne sped through a yellow light. Only one more street to go and she'd be at practice and would secure her spot as captain of the Palm Desert varsity tennis team.

Jayne hazarded a glance at the clock. 4:02. *Crap!* "Sure. I'll call Grams later tonight."

"Great. You're the best oldest daughter I've ever had." Her mom hung up. Gen Thompkins wasn't big into saying good-byes.

Jayne was about to put the phone down when it rang again.

This time she looked at the caller ID. *Ellie.* She flipped open the phone. As annoyed as she was at Ellie, taking the call was an automatic reflex. Like breathing.

She looked up from the caller ID and a cold sweat broke out over her body. The intersection was ten, maybe fifteen yards away. The light was red.

She was barreling toward it.

And the red sedan in the middle of the intersection.

5

OH MY GOD.

Oh. My. God.

Jayne's head was resting on something weird. Actually, her head resting on anything right now was weird. She slowly sat up and realized it was the car's air bag.

White dust moved in slow motion around her. The smell of burned rubber filled her nostrils.

She felt like she was watching a bad made-for-TV movie. And some stupid girl answering a cell phone had gotten into an accident.

A pain shot through her wrist. The girl wasn't on TV. It was her. Her, Jayne Thompkins, the girl who never even got so much as a detention. *She* was the stupid girl in the crushed car.

She turned to watch the dust from the air bag float through the air and took a deep, quivering breath.

"Oww!" Her nose throbbed, like a brick had slammed into it.

She followed one of the dust particles with her eyes and tried to remember what had happened. Everything had been such a blur, followed by screeching brakes, shattering glass, crunching metal.

She sat in the car and waited for the ringing in her ears to stop. Jayne heard a voice coming from below her. Why would a voice be coming from that direction? She tried to make sense of it, but her brain felt like it was in a bowl of really dense Jell-O.

The cell phone. She'd hit TALK right before she'd seen the red light. The red car.

Then black as her face smashed into the air bag.

Where was the red car? It wasn't in front of her, or to her left, either.

It was to her right, locked together with a black luxury car. The black car's hood had mangled the red one's. Both front air bags were visible in the red sedan.

Jayne's heartbeat sounded abnormally loud in her ears, and it felt like her stomach was being wrung like a wet dish towel.

She closed her eyes and the images replayed in her head.

Her white Jetta plowing into the red sedan. Pushing it into oncoming traffic. A black blur smashing into the sedan. Head-on.

Jayne opened her eyes, even though she just wanted to keep them closed and rewind time. She scanned the distance between her and the other two cars. About thirty yards separated her from the destruction she'd caused.

Oh God.

"Are you okay?" A man with a Diamondbacks baseball hat was tapping on her side window, his eyebrows high and his eyes wide with concern. Jayne pushed the button to lower the window, but it didn't work. *That's because the car's dead, idiot.*

"Just unlock it." He pointed at the door.

Jayne nodded mutely and did just that. He opened the car and crouched down beside her. She numbly looked at the small tear running along the bill of his cap.

"Just stay here and try not to move. My wife's already called 911 for you and the other cars." He pointed to the Circle K behind him. "We were filling up and saw everything."

She took a shallow breath through her mouth so her nose wouldn't hurt. As she sat there, hearing everything but not really understanding anything, she heard her name being called from below her. Again, and again.

Numbly, not really thinking about what she was doing, Jayne started to reach down again. But her seat belt didn't have any give to it and kept her immobile.

"My cell phone." She forced herself to form the words. Had talking always been this hard? "Could you get it for me? It's under my feet."

Once Mr. Diamondbacks found the phone, he handed it to her.

"Jayne! Jaynie, are you okay? Please, Jaynie, please talk to me!"

"I'm here, Ellie." Jayne closed her eyes, every single pore in her body aching.

"What happened? It sounded like you crashed." Ellie was sobbing through the words. "Did you crash?"

Annoyance washed over Jayne. She usually felt this way

when someone asked a dumb question in class. And Ellie's question definitely qualified as a dumb one. Jayne reached for the words she needed to say. It was time to come out of this waking coma. "I've been in a car accident. I need you to call Mom and Dad. Use their cell numbers."

Jayne continued to list what needed to be done. Feed her dog, Britney. Call Coach to tell him she wasn't going to make practice. Call Brendan with Key Club to tell him she couldn't make the meeting tonight. She turned the phone away from her mouth. "Sir, what's the closest hospital around here?"

"Camelback Regional."

Jayne put the phone in front of her mouth again. "Tell Mom they'll probably be taking me to Camelback Regional."

Ellie was sniffling and didn't answer.

"Ellie, are you listening?" Her sister was never good in a crisis. Just like the time Ellie misplaced her freshman lit take-home midterm and she dissolved into a puddle on the kitchen floor. It was Jayne who found it ten minutes later in the middle of a stack of *Vogue*s in Ellie's room. "Camelback. Regional. Write this down before you forget."

Jayne heard a snot-filled sniff and then, "Camelback Regional. Got it." Another sniff. "God, Jayne, what happened?"

For an instant, another flash of annoyance streaked through Jayne. She didn't have time to hold Ellie's hand. "I need to go now. Remember, feed Britney. Call Coach. Call Brendan. And tell Mom and Dad Camelback Regional."

She hung up before Ellie could ask anything else. For a second, she felt like her mom.

She hadn't wasted time saying good-bye.

Jayne dropped the phone onto the passenger seat. *Stupid friggin' phone. I would've seen the light if I hadn't answered it.*

Would've, could've, should've.

"Hey, you still with me here?" The guy in the baseball hat was leaning into the car again. For the first time, she realized he smelled like BO.

"The people that are in the other cars. Are they okay?" *Please. Please.*

Please.

"My wife's checking on them." The guy pulled up the hem of his T-shirt. "You have some blood coming out of your nose. I'm going to wipe it away, okay?"

She nodded and leaned back in the seat.

He hesitated. "You don't have AIDS or anything, right?"

She shook her head and looked in the rearview mirror. Her nose seemed different. And not just bloody. "Do you think I broke it?"

Did anyone else break anything? The thought shot through her brain.

"Yeah. Looks that way."

Jayne took the news in. She grabbed onto the idea of a broken nose. It seemed a lot less scary than the other thoughts scrambling through her brain. "Do they always hurt so much? Broken noses, I mean."

"Afraid so." He pointed to his own nose. It hooked to the right. "I've had three breaks myself."

"Tim! I need you over here!"

Jayne looked over the inflated air bag in front of her and

saw a thirtyish mom-type waving for the man next to her.

"I'll be back in a sec, okay?" He dropped the hem of his shirt, Jayne's blood peppering the bottom, and made his way to the other car. Hesitantly, Jayne focused again on the cars entwined in front of her.

A gray-haired man had gotten out of the black car and was on his cell phone. He looked like a business guy in his black trousers and blue button-down. He seemed fine. His voice certainly was, based on how loud he was talking about "the goddamn accident I've just been in."

One down. One to go.

Over in the red car, a woman still sat behind the steering wheel. All Jayne could make out was a messy ponytail and two inches of black roots. The woman was leaning down to look at something in the passenger side—the side that Jayne had hit.

The woman's head rose for the span of one raspy, mouth-inhaled breath. The woman's eyes spanned across the passenger seat, the passenger-seat window, and the crumpled hood of Jayne's two-month-old car.

The woman looked back down as quickly as she had looked up.

But not before Jayne saw terror.

Panic—way worse than anything she'd ever felt before a test or driving to tennis five minutes late—started eating away at Jayne's stomach. She unclicked her seat belt and tried to pull herself out the open door. What was in the passenger seat? *Who* was in the passenger seat?

The air bag pressed her against the seat, though, and she

shifted her body to get by. The movement jarred her left arm, and it felt like a red-hot poker had been shoved through her wrist. Nausea washed over her and tears filled her eyes.

She blinked her eyelids like hummingbird wings. *Stop crying. Stop. You caused this. No one here needs to see you in "poor me" mode.* She licked her lips and tasted the tears that had made their way there.

Salty. Tears are made of salt, right? She plundered her mind for the answer. Her anatomy class during her freshman year had covered the composition of tears. She tried to remember the list of ingredients. *Salt is sodium. So sodium. What else . . . potassium? Yeah. Potassium, glucose . . .*

Jayne had made it as far as "glucose" when two motorcycle cops rolled up to the intersection. One started directing traffic while the other one darted a look at Jayne. He took a step in her direction, but then hesitated when the Diamondbacks couple called him over.

He gave her a thumbs-up, a question in his eyes. *Are you okay?* he seemed to be asking. Jayne attempted a smile. He nodded and headed for the red sedan.

"Honey, are you okay?"

Jayne jerked, hearing the words she'd just thought in her head being said aloud. She turned to see a middle-aged woman with a red visor. The logo in the center matched the gas station's behind her. "I saw the accident from the store. It looked like a bad one."

State the obvious much? Whoa, where'd that come from? Jayne struggled to get her emotions under control. This woman was trying to be nice. She smelled like hot dogs and stale cigarettes, but that wasn't her fault.

Well, maybe the stale cigarette part.

"Do you know how the people in the red car are?" The question kept rearing its head, and now Jayne got to ask it again. She hadn't talked to anyone since the guy in the baseball cap, and now here was a lady with big, brown, puppy-dog eyes pooled up with sympathy.

"It looks like it's a mom and her little girl in there."

"Little girl?" Jayne started taking more shallow, shaky breaths. The sympathy in this woman's eyes was putting her over the edge. Not the throbbing in her nose and wrist. Not the stiffness settling into her neck. Not whatever was happening in the other car.

Jayne tried to look into the next car, but she still couldn't see anything. The driver now stood beside it, her hand shielding her eyes from the sun. She was shifting from one foot from the other, chewing on an acrylic thumbnail on her other hand. The cop who'd given Jayne the thumbs-up was now leaning over the driver's seat and concentrating on whoever was in the passenger side.

Not whoever, Jayne. A little girl. A little girl is sitting there. Or lying there.

Or suffering there.

"Yeah. I'd put her at maybe five, six years old." The woman attempted a comforting smile, but it didn't quite work. The tears in her eyes were the giveaway.

Jayne continued taking shallow breaths through her mouth

as the tears ran down her cheeks. She didn't even try to stop them.

"Is sh-she okay?"

The clerk looked past Jayne, avoiding her eyes. "I don't think so, hon."

6

ROOM 208, RIGHT?"

Jayne opened her eyes as she heard her mom's no-nonsense voice in the hallway. She'd been dozing on and off thanks to whatever drugs they were pumping through her IV, and her mind was fuzzy around the edges.

The fuzziness was a good thing. It was helping her forget about the sound of squealing tires, breaking glass, and crunching metal. The smell of burned rubber. The tiny flecks of dust from the air bag.

The red car and the woman with the look of terror on her face.

The paramedics had arrived soon after the motorcycle cops. They'd put Jayne into the ambulance before she had had a chance to figure out what was going on with the red car. Or the little girl.

Jayne pushed the memories aside. The neck brace kept her from looking anywhere but straight, thanks to a slight case of whiplash. A splint was taped to her nose, which had been reset by the docs here. Her left arm was immobilized from her fingers to her elbow thanks to a broken wrist.

She looked disinterestedly at the tray that had been placed at the foot of the bed. It held a bowl of green Jell-O and a yellow plastic cup holding a straw and what had to be lukewarm water.

She hadn't touched either. She had no appetite. And she wasn't thirsty enough to want to move and test the effectiveness of the pain meds.

Gen Thompkins pushed through the door, her face perfect in its on-camera makeup and the dim light of the room. Her face had a studied look of concern, like the kind she wore when she talked to teenagers who drowned their babies.

For a second, Jayne wondered if she was now in the same league as baby-drowners.

The click of her mother's stilettos sounded loud in the small, sterile room. Jayne looked at the clock by the wall-mounted TV. It was 9:02. Shelly from the morning show must've been filling in for Arizona's number-one Emmy-winning newscaster.

"Good, you're awake."

In the dim light of the room, her mom looked like the local celebrity she was. Her face was poreless, her eyes were enhanced to be greener, and her lips were perfectly plumped—just enough to make viewers wonder whether they were natural or not. (They were not.)

The only difference tonight was that Gen's eyes and the edge of her nose looked a little red. Which was weird. Jayne's mom was usually really good at making sure her foundation and powder covered the telltale signs of her spring allergies.

"Hi." Jayne smoothed a strand of blonde hair behind an ear. Her hand brushed the ponytail at the nape of her neck. She slipped off the elastic band and smoothed out the tangles. There was no point in keeping it in. It wasn't like she was going to tennis practice today. Or tomorrow. Or the rest of this season.

Based on what the doctor had told her, she'd be sidelined for the next six weeks. She'd be getting her cast off just in time for summer vacation. Or, in Jayne's case, summer school.

Jayne listened to the clock ticking across the room, letting her thoughts drift. Summer school. It seemed so far away. So . . . not important.

"The doctor told me your broke your nose and your wrist." Her mom sat on the bed, unbuttoning her turquoise blazer as she did so.

"Yeah. The air bag did that." She slowly lifted her good hand and touched the neck brace with her fingertips. Her eyelids felt heavy. Sleep sounded good right now. "Whiplash, too. And the car. I broke the car."

"We'll talk about the car later, when you're more lucid. They're still giving you pain medication, right?" Her mom's eyes narrowed, as if to gauge the truth for herself. Ever the vigilant journalist; that was Gen Thompkins.

"Yeah." *They're the best invention ever.* But she didn't say that. Not with her mom scrutinizing her like she was a frog with its guts pinned open.

She concentrated on a strand of hair that was flipping out from her mom's blonde bob while all the others flipped under. *Gen Thompkins is going to find you and tame you, little hair.* "Is Dad with you?"

Her mom pulled the covers over Jayne's waist, folding them back and smoothing the edges over her lap.

"He's on his way up from Tucson."

Jayne tried to figure out what day of the week it was. It felt like a week had passed, not just—she looked at the clock by the TV and slowly did the math—five hours.

"That's right. Today's Tuesday. Teaching that herb class down in Tucson." Jayne pictured her dad in his hybrid, speeding toward Phoenix. Scratch that. He always drove ten miles *under* the speed limit.

Jayne pulled the blanket away from her mom's hands. *Enough with the blanket rearranging already.* She took a minute to catch her breath. Exertion was not a good thing with these pain meds coursing through her system. She was getting sleepier by the minute. "Where's Ellie?"

"At home. She fought me tooth and nail about coming, but I told her that you'd probably be out of it with the drugs they're pumping into you. Looks like I was right." Her mom got up and took the water cup from the tray. "Have some water, Jayne. If your dad was here, he'd tell you it makes a body heal faster."

Gen smiled at this last part. It was a weird smile, though. Like her mind was on other things. Like trying to figure out how to smile without cracking her makeup.

Jayne obediently took the cup. It would've taken more energy to argue with her mom than to just take a quick sip of the plastic-flavored water.

"Please don't. Bring Ellie here, I mean." She handed the cup back to her mom. For a second, she thought she saw four Gen Thompkinses. She blinked and they merged back into one.

Jayne really didn't want to think about Ellie. She didn't know why. Maybe . . . maybe . . . She tried to swim through the fog in order to figure it out. The answer was just out of reach, but her gut told her: Keep Ellie at arm's length.

She trusted her gut; it was usually right.

Her mom fiddled with the straw in the water cup, tapping the end against the sides of the plastic.

"Jayne." Her mom stopped to clear her throat. She put the cup on the nightstand and met Jayne's eyes. "I spoke to one of the police officers who was at the scene of your accident."

Jayne struggled to keep her eyes open.

"Officer Bradley. He told me he'll set up an appointment to talk to you after you're off the painkillers. He needs you as clear-headed as possible before he takes your statement."

Gen smoothed a strand of golden blonde hair behind an ear. "When he does, I'll make sure our lawyer's there."

Jayne tried to make sense out of her mom's words. "Why do I need a lawyer? I caused the accident, right? That means it's no one's fault but mine. Right?"

She halfway hoped her mom would correct her. That her brakes had failed or the woman in the other car had crashed into her. Neither of those scenarios made sense, but something inside Jayne made her hope something—or someone—other than her was at fault.

"It's a precaution, Jayne."

A precaution. Against what? Jayne couldn't think of the answer. She didn't want to ask her mom to explain, either. She was afraid of what she might hear.

As her mind wandered, Jayne remembered the French test

she had next week. Fifty vocab words about what a person could find at a museum. She didn't know where that thought had come from, but she held on to it for dear life. She wanted to think about something else. Something other than . . .

"Am I getting out soon?" What was she, a prisoner? She added, "Out of the hospital, I mean."

"I've convinced the doctor to keep you here an additional twenty-four hours."

Jayne knew what that was shorthand for: Gen Thompkins had given her "Do you know who I am" speech at Camelback Regional.

"I want to make sure you have a clean bill of health, especially since I've covered so many stories where a person seemed perfectly fine after a crash and *boom*"—she clapped her hands together—"they die from an undiscovered blood clot."

A whole day that would be filled with nothing but her thoughts while she waited for a blood clot to show up. The French test popped into Jayne's head again.

"I'm going to need my French book. Could you bring that tomorrow? In the morning?"

"That's what I like to hear." Her mom reached down and briefly squeezed Jayne's hand. "A girl who's got her eyes on the prize. I'll have Diane bring by your books tomorrow."

Diane. Diane. Oh, yeah. Gen's assistant. The one who was supposed to assist her at work. Not at home.

Jayne felt like someone was holding her eyelids down. She struggled to open them again and found her mother looking behind her at the clock. "I need to get going. Diane's babysitting Ellie, but she can't stay for long. She still needs to do some research for me."

Diane is "babysitting" Ellie? Such a classic Gen move. A semi-hysterical laugh filled Jayne's head.

Before she totally gave in to the pills, Jayne mumbled, "The little girl. In the red car. Is she okay?"

She was almost asleep before she realized her mother had finally started talking. "The driver is fine. She has a slight concussion and that's about it. The little girl . . . the little girl is on a ventilator. The doctors say she has a broken neck."

Jayne forced her eyes open. She knew she should be feeling bad. Crying, even. She had caused an accident. A car accident. She'd never done anything so horrible in her life. Ever.

But the drugs were working against her and her eyes slid shut again. Her mother said something about the air bag hitting the girl. Something about the girl being six. Something else about the thoughtless mother who'd put her kid in the front seat without a seat belt on.

Jayne didn't hear anything else. The drugs had finally won. She stopped struggling and slept.

And she dreamed. About red cars. About men with baseball hats.

About little girls with angel wings.

7

Jayne stared at the flat screen and then clicked it off. It was one of the few things she'd fought for when her mother redid her room freshman year. Her mom had wanted her to have an environment that would help her concentrate on homework. Jayne had argued that TV helped her study . . . and the Discovery Channel was research. Her mom had capitulated, but only if Jayne promised to take down her posters of Mary-Kate and Ashley, bull's-eyes etched onto each of their foreheads with a ballpoint pen.

They'd been replaced with framed black-and-white pictures of Audrey Hepburn.

Jayne had hidden her scowl when her mom's decorator had picked them out. As if Jayne, at five foot eleven and perfectly happy in jeans and a T-shirt, could ever even hope to simulate Audrey Hepburn's look.

She dropped the remote on the white carpet and pulled the queen-size down comforter over her head, encasing herself in an igloo of white cotton and goose down.

Today the room felt like a cold crypt, a shell that didn't house a teenage girl with a French test next week and a completed paper on post-colonialism on her desk (done two weeks ahead of schedule).

She wasn't the same girl who'd written that paper. The girl who had once argued in ninth-grade debate why cell phones were the downfall of civilization.

Now she was someone who'd put a little girl in the hospital, attached to tubes and IVs. Now she was a footnote for someone else's debate on the downfall of civilization.

Today was day five since the accident. A Saturday. A day usually filled with ten hours of studying and going to All the Sweet Tomorrows with Ellie. Sharing a sugarless Sinful Chocolate Cheesecake Cupcake. Coming back home, still on a sucralose high, and finishing up a paper or reading another three chapters for a test.

Right now, her brain didn't care. She couldn't study if she wanted to.

Instead, she was busy thinking about her white Jetta crashing into that red car. The nice guy in the Diamondbacks hat checking on her. The woman with a look of horror on her face as she concentrated on who was in the passenger seat. Paramedics and cops arriving. The Circle K lady staying with Jayne. The cigarette smell coming off her shirt and hair, making Jayne sick.

Forcing her eyes shut, she concentrated on turning off the broken record. Car crash. Nice man. Woman with terrified look. Cops. Paramedics. Circle K woman.

God, she needed more pills. Not for the pain. That was under control.

For the memories.

"Jaynie? Can I come in?"

This was the fifth time her dad had come by today. And it wasn't even ten A.M.

She'd been avoiding him since he'd come back from Tucson. Especially after she found out he'd taken some personal days to stay with her. She didn't need a babysitter. She wasn't Ellie.

It was hard to be around him right now. He had picked up the habit of talking to her in low, soft tones, like she was going to break. Sometimes it felt like she was, there was so much pressure building up inside of her. Wondering what was going to happen next.

Luckily, the painkillers kept her from thinking too much about it.

She pushed down the comforter, sucking in a breath of cool, clean air. Sean Thompkins wasn't bad. He was the most even-tempered person she'd ever known. The perfect foil for his high-stress wife, most days. Anyway, at least *he* wasn't pretending like nothing had happened. Ellie and her mom, on the other hand, were acting like everything was fine. Like the world was fine.

Like Jayne was fine.

Jayne sat up, awkwardly pulling her European history book off the floor with her one good hand, flipping to a random page. "Yeah, come in."

Her dad opened the door, his body still hidden from view.

"Hey. I was thinking about going to Blockbuster. You want anything?"

Her dad was pretty good-looking as far as dads went. Lanky and tan with messy spikes of brown hair, he had light blue eyes, a feature Ellie shared with him. Both of the girls had gotten his brown hair, until Gen had turned the sisters white-blonde two years ago during their annual mother-daughters spa trip.

She shook her head, staring blindly at an illustration of D-day. "No thanks. Gotta study."

"Not even one of those chick flicks you like to watch with Ellie?" He winked at her. "I'll even get you one you've seen before."

This isn't me with the chicken pox, bored and watching Never Been Kissed *for the fiftieth time. Being sick gets movies in bed. Being the girl responsible for putting a little girl on life support gets . . . gets . . .*

She didn't know what broken bones and a car crash got her. Definitely not a chick flick.

"You want some company, then?"

"I really need to study, Dad." She started blindly reading the page in front of her.

"No time even for a furry visitor?"

He walked into the room holding a squirming pug, her black face scrunched up more than usual as she tried to get down. A white cone encircled the dog's neck, making her face look like the center of one pissed-off flower.

Jayne dropped the book on the floor and put her hands out. "When'd Britney get back from the vet?"

Her dad put the pug in her lap, and a warm wet tongue swathed her face. "About two minutes ago. Diane brought her over."

Jayne scrubbed the dog's belly with her good hand while bopping Britney's nose with the fingers protruding from her cast. The dog was pretty energetic after getting eight stitches thanks to her run-in with Mrs. Allison's tabby.

Right then, Jayne felt normal. Like it was five days ago, pre-accident, with the only worry in the world being the French test.

"So, kid."

Crap. Her dad saying "kid" was never a good conversation starter. It usually preceded stuff like, "We don't think playing four sports this year is going to be good for your emotional welfare."

"I was thinking we could go see Larry next week."

Larry . . . Larry? Oh, God. *Larry!* She forced a smile and rubbed a small eye-booger out of Britney's eye. *Think fast, Jaynie girl.* "I'm good. No reason to waste his time with my sob story."

Her dad sat on the edge of her bed and pinched the toes of one foot, shaking it back and forth. "I think seeing him will help, Jaynie. Talking to a family friend with a psychology degree might be easier than talking to your mom and me right now."

Exactly. A family friend who'd report back to his friends.

Her dad shook his head, as if he was reading her thoughts. "The things you tell him will be strictly confidential." He crossed his heart with a finger. "I swear."

Even if she did agree to meet with Larry, she didn't know how seriously she could take him. He was a long-haired hippie who dressed and acted like Woodstock had just happened a week ago. He smelled like patchouli and liked to decorate with Buddhas. He kind of looked like a Buddha, with his male-pattern baldness and the pregnant-looking tummy those loose-fitting Hawaiian shirts didn't hide too well.

Ellie had nicknamed him Larry the Fairy because the only thing he ever talked about was feelings, like a girl.

Jayne sure didn't want to share anything, much less her feelings, with Larry. She didn't even know *what* she was feeling. And if she didn't know, how was *he* going to know?

"Can I see how I feel next week?" She scratched Britney's belly. She didn't want to go to counseling. That meant she had to talk about what happened. She didn't even want to *think* about what happened, much less talk about it. "I have a lot of class work to catch up on."

"Sure, sure." If that smile was any broader, her dad would've cracked his face in half. "Well, I guess I'll leave you alone. Ellie and I will go get a movie and takeout. Any requests?"

Jayne shook her head. "I'm good. Thanks."

He kissed Jayne on the forehead and left, keeping the door cracked two inches.

Jayne dragged herself from the bed and closed the door the rest of the way, then locked it. She went back to bed, pulled the covers up, and pressed her nose into Britney's fur.

There was four days' worth of homework waiting for her, as well as that French test to study for. She willed herself to care.

She didn't.

"Jayne, phone!" Ellie rattled the doorknob. "What's with the locked door?"

Jayne pried her eyes open and saw it was 6:12. Her room was brighter and warmer. She might've gotten the bigger room, but at least Ellie didn't have to deal with a window that faced west as the afternoon sun hovered on the horizon.

"Who is it?" She wasn't up to talking to Tom. He'd already left three messages with her dad. She hadn't turned on her computer in the last couple of days, but she was sure she'd find a few e-mails from him, too.

He was persistent, she'd give him that. Which was part of the reason he'd lasted as her friend for so long. All the others had gotten sick of her always studying and not being the typical teenage girl who would talk on the phone two hours every day.

"It's Mr. Reynolds."

As in Coach Reynolds. Did she want to talk to him? She rubbed between Britney's ears. Her wrist and nose hurt, which meant the painkillers were wearing off. At least she wouldn't be loopy talking to him.

In her gut, she knew what the topic of conversation was going to be.

"I'll use the phone in here." She hadn't heard the phone ring because she always kept the ringer off. That way she didn't lose her concentration when she was in the middle of a trigonometry equation. Jayne picked up the phone and covered the mouthpiece before hitting the TALK button. "Hang up, Ellie!"

Once she heard the click, Jayne spoke. She tried to make her voice sound like it usually did. Confident. "Hi, Coach."

"Good to hear your voice, Jayne. I just wanted to see if you were okay after, uh, the other day."

"I'm doing good." Even in her current state, she couldn't let her grammar mistake go by uncorrected. "I mean I'm doing well, thank you."

"Heard you hurt your arm?"

"Yeah. Well, the wrist. My nose is in a splint, but that should go away in a couple of weeks." The neck brace had been more annoying than helpful and now sat in the dark under her bed.

"I wish you could finish out the season with us. Especially since this would've been the first year we had a junior be captain *and* first seed."

She felt something hot and prickly in her eyes. She blinked, willing the tears to go away. "Yeah, me too. But there's always next year, right?"

"Exactly. Next year." Coach cleared his throat. "So, Jayne, I wanted you to hear it from me first before you read it in the *Javelina*."

Since Jayne was the features editor, she knew exactly what he was about to tell her. Her throat closed up and she felt her nose start to run. *You will not cry. You will* not *cry. You deserve this.* "What's that, Coach Reynolds?"

"I made Missy captain."

She knew the words were coming. They still hurt all the same, though.

"Anyway, with everything you're going through, this whole captain business probably isn't high on your list of priorities, right?" He laughed, and it sounded nervous.

Jayne felt the room start to close in on her. She got up and opened the blinds.

Across the street, the Travises' minivan was coated with dust. Someone had etched GO JAVELINAS! on the back window. Judy Travis had been her partner in chemistry, but Judy'd had a bad habit of whispering when the teacher was talking. Jayne had eventually lied to Mrs. Pollock about a draft from the air conditioner and early-onset arthritis and had been moved four seats over.

"You there, Jayne?"

"Yeah." At least she didn't feel like crying right now. She was too busy thinking about normal teenagers. And how she'd been trying so hard for so long not to be one of them.

"You okay with everything?"

For a second, she thought he was talking about her life. No, she wasn't okay. But she wasn't about to use Coach as a phone counselor. The man taught history and wore the same gym shorts in two different colors to class every day. "I'm good, Coach. Really."

"Good, good." He cleared his throat again, a lengthy affair that made her hold the phone a few inches from her ear. "I'm still at the tennis courts. We had a match against Central. Won all but one of the matches."

He paused, like he was waiting for Jayne to congratulate him. What did she care?

There was a girl hooked to a ventilator. Because of her. Tennis matches weren't that important in comparison.

"Well, I better get going," Coach said. "Mrs. Reynolds needs some foil for a chicken she's baking tonight. I'll see you in the halls on Monday?"

Jayne ran a finger over the flat surface of one white blind. She listened with half an ear to the tinny sound it made. "Sounds good. I'll see you then."

As she hung up, she slowly closed the blinds, shutting out the world and a car proclaiming, GO JAVELINAS!

8

Have you seen my medic alert bracelet?"

Jayne pushed her scrambled eggs into the bacon, making them touch and ignoring Ellie and yet another of Ellie's demands. Ellie wanting eggs. Dad making Ellie's eggs. The eggs being runny and inedible.

Just like Ellie liked them.

"No, I have not." Now that the eggs were touching the meat, she didn't have to put up a front about eating them. Even her mother knew she didn't eat food that touched.

Today was the first day she'd be back in school. Jayne concentrated on smushing the eggs down, pushing the liquid yolk out of the gelatinous mound. Right now, getting the liquid squeezed out of her eggs was her number-one priority.

It kept her from thinking about . . . other things.

Which wasn't realistic. Not while she was sitting here already sweating in the navy trousers and white blouse her mom had picked out for her. The outfit she'd wear to see the lawyer after school.

There was no reason to think. Not with the notebook of questions her mom had painstakingly dictated to Diane. Questions Jayne had spent three hours answering late last night to keep her mind off the pile of books with a week's worth of undone homework in them.

Her mom had edited her answers, too. Like the question that asked, "Were you distracted when you were driving?" In place of the paragraph where she'd detailed checking her cell-phone caller ID, her mom had scratched through her words and had written, "Just the usual amount of distraction a driver faces from day to day."

"Are you even listening to me?"

Jayne looked up at Ellie. Her life was so simple, and it didn't hurt any that she looked like a movie star in the making. Her skin was as flawless as Kate Winslet's or some other English actress's.

Jayne? She was fighting a losing battle with an angry, bulbous stress pimple on her right cheek. Reminiscent of the vicious pimples those *Survivor* people got after three weeks without soap or Proactiv.

"Why don't you just use your backup bracelet?" Jayne concentrated on the food in front of her, never having felt less hungry in her life.

She had exactly eight hours and thirty-seven minutes until she met with the lawyer. Until she found out how much more her life was going to change. Which was a weird concept for a girl who'd planned every aspect of her life since she was three.

From when Ken and Barbie were ready to get married, to which college Jayne would eventually apply to.

She went to the sink and scraped her untouched breakfast into the garbage disposal, careful not to let her cast get wet. Ellie stood next to her, frantically looking through a pile of *Arizona Republic*s.

Jayne rolled her eyes as the eggs slipped down the drain. "The bracelet's probably in your gym locker."

Ellie started pulling open kitchen drawers, rifling through their organized contents. "Why do you say that?"

Jayne stifled a sigh as she went over to a kitchen chair to zip up her messenger bag. "Because that's where you've left it at least two other times."

She took one last look inside her bag. French book, chemistry book, *The Scarlet Letter*. Everything she needed was there for her first day back at school.

Whoopee.

She straightened and saw her belt buckle wasn't centered with her shirt buttons. She didn't bother doing anything about it. Or the cuff that had come undone on her right pant leg. Jayne just wanted to be in her pj's. That sounded good about now. So did popping a few of those pain pills, taking a marathon nap, and snuggling with Britney. Life would be perfect if she could just stay home.

Okay, maybe not perfect, but at least she'd be away from the real world. Where people knew about . . . Where people knew. Thanks to the midday, five o'clock, six o'clock, and nine o'clock news.

Jayne sat down and looked at the clock. It was time to go. Time to get the day over with. "Where's Dad?"

Ellie had given up her bracelet search and was leaning against the kitchen counter, eating M&M's. She shrugged. "Dunno." She dumped the last M&M into her mouth. "Don't tell Dad I can't find it. He'll write his number on me in Magic Marker or something."

A week ago, Jayne would've lectured Ellie about eating that candy crap. It wasn't good for her diabetes.

It also wasn't good for her diabetes to be going outside without her bracelet after eating a handful of M&M's.

Today, though, Jayne sat down and put her forehead on top of her crossed arms.

She heard the jingle jangle of pocket change a few seconds before her dad rushed in. She lifted her head, the movement cracking her neck. God, she was tense.

Her dad took a traveler's mug out of the cupboard. "Good, you're both here." He filled the mug with the green iced tea he'd made the night before. "I was hung up on a conference call with U of A."

He looked around, patting his blazer's pockets. "Insulin. Did Jaynie give you your shot, Ellie?"

Ellie shook her head. "Not yet. She's been too busy getting ready for school."

Jayne wanted to put her head back down on her arms and shut out her sister. Whatever. Ellie had had plenty of time to ask her. She was just being self-centered, like always.

Like Gen.

Jayne didn't say anything as she went to the fridge. On top

of everything else going on today, she didn't want to get into an argument with Ellie. On autopilot, like she'd done a thousand times before, she pulled out a vial and started rolling it with her good hand against the side of her leg, mixing together the milky liquid inside.

"I'll swab the decks, Captain." Their dad mock-saluted Ellie and took a cotton ball out of the jar by the fridge and soaked it with the bottle of rubbing alcohol beside it. "Where are we doing this one today?"

Ellie pulled down her waistband a few inches on her left hip. She looked up at the kitchen light. "You almost ready, Jayne?"

Her back to her dad and sister, Jayne pressed her lips together. Ellie was begging for a fight. The little jerk wasn't going to get one, though.

After checking the syringe for air bubbles, Jayne pinched the flesh at Ellie's hip and pushed the needle into the skin. Ever since her sister had been diagnosed with juvenile diabetes at age six, it had fallen on either their dad or, in the last four years or so, Jayne to give Ellie the shot three times a day. At school, the nurse did it.

No one else could do it, though. Or rather, would do it. Their mom's gag reflex activated whenever she saw a needle, and Ellie couldn't stomach giving herself the shot.

Their dad gave Ellie a fresh cotton ball with alcohol to clean up the tiny dot of blood from the puncture. Jayne threw the used syringe into a lidded plastic container and wondered what the garbage men must think of them. Did they think they were a bunch of drug addicts?

With everything else that had happened recently, Jayne could just imagine the headlines if one of the local networks saw their trash. *Jayne Thompkins Turns to Drugs to Forget Tragedy!*

If she had been another kind of girl—an average, wimpy girl—maybe she'd turn to drugs. But she was Jayne Lee Thompkins: straight-A, Harvard-bound Jayne Lee Thompkins.

She didn't do that kind of thing.

9

THere were cameras in front of the school.

There. Were. Cameras.

Jayne started to scoot down in her seat. She wanted to slide down to the floor. But she didn't. In fact, she straightened up. She had never hidden from anyone. Ever. Then again, she'd never done anything in her life that she had to hide from.

"Jayne!" One of the vultures with a mike had seen her. He started walking toward her like a man working out on a treadmill. One by one, the rest of the reporters realized where he was heading and followed. With that same quick, determined stride.

Holy crap.

"Jesus." That word coming from her dad was unexpected. He rarely swore. "Your mother and I were hoping they wouldn't be here."

"Oh my God." Ellie pulled against Jayne's seat, leaning over and looking out the front windshield. "There are so many freakin' cameras! Does my hair look all right?"

"Why are *they* here?" Jayne felt her stomach clench, and she willed herself not to puke up the two bites of eggs that had gone down there.

Her dad let out a long breath. "Probably because they couldn't get near you at the house."

Since Jayne had gotten home, the news vans had been at the end of the driveway, off their property. The vultures knew they couldn't push their legal boundaries when it came to the queen of all vultures.

But they'd gone away after a couple of days. They'd gotten their shots of the house, the background for their news stories. So why were they here?

"But I'm old news."

"For anyone else, you would be." Her dad's voice was calm. Soothing. Just like it always was. "But you're a bright, pretty girl who got some bad luck thrown her way. And you need to keep in mind that you're Gen Thompkins's daughter. They probably want to get an on-air comment to take her down a notch or two."

He turned and grinned at her. "At least your mom dressed you up today, right?"

Jayne knew he was trying to make her feel better. Instead, he was making her feel like a special-needs person. *At least your mom dressed you up today.*

"Do you want me to drive to another entrance? Or maybe come back later?"

"Yeah, Jayne, let's ditch." Ellie was still pulling at her seat. Jayne was feeling dizzy from the movement.

"No, we're not ditching." The sooner this day got started, the sooner it would be over. "I'll just keep my head up and my eyes forward."

That's what her mother had taught her. "Guilty, shameful people look at the ground, Jayne. If you're ever in trouble, act like the queen of England. Otherwise you're going to be judged and executed by the public."

Her mom had told her this when she was seven and about to welcome the parents to parent-teacher night on behalf of the first grade.

She opened the door, keeping a hand knotted around the strap of her book bag. "Come on, Ellie."

"Wait." Her dad had grabbed Jayne's wrist.

"Yeah?"

"I don't know. I don't know what to do. I know that's an undadlike thing to say, but these people"—he nodded toward the reporters, who were about five seconds from the car—"are going to eat us alive."

If she was a lesser person, she would've turned tail and headed home.

But she wasn't that kind of person. Then again, it might've been easier if she *was* that type of person.

"I just want to get this over with." She turned toward the backseat. "Ellie, get your bag, stay close, and don't answer any of their questions. Got it?"

Jayne opened the door without waiting for a reply and plastered a small smile on her face. In the distance, she saw the principal making his way down the steps.

The vultures screamed, "Jayne, Jayne!"

She heard her name but everything else was a jumble of words. The ten or so reporters were talking over one another. She kept the smile in place. *Forty yards. I can make it that far. Just keep heading straight and don't say anything.*

One of the reporters, a woman who was on the network that

came in second after Jayne's mom's, shoved a mike about two inches from her nose. "Jayne, how do you feel after hearing the news?"

Hearing the news? After watching it? What was this woman yammering about?

The woman had a follow-up: "How do you feel knowing six-year-old Brenda Deavers is brain-dead?"

Brain-dead? Jayne's feet stopped working and she came to a standstill. Cameras flashed around her. But she didn't see them. That little girl was on a ventilator. Jayne hadn't heard anything about her brain being . . . dead.

She didn't have an answer for this lady. She didn't have an answer, period. But she had questions. A lot of questions.

"Jayne." Ellie hissed the word in her ear. "Jayne, get going. C'mon."

She had to get to the library. To the computers. Computers always had the answers if you searched them correctly.

And she was a master researcher.

Jayne slowly started walking again as she focused on the front doors. As she did, a tiny voice chanted.

Brain-dead. Brain-dead. Brain-dead.

The first-period bell had already rung by the time Jayne made it through the double doors. Behind her, she heard the principal shout, "You're not allowed on school grounds. Get off my campus!"

She beelined it toward the library.

"Jayne!" Ellie had stopped in front of the door to her classroom. "Isn't your homeroom down the other hall?"

"Yep." But she wasn't going there.

Her dress shoes, a respectable pair of two-inch pumps, clicked down the hallway, away from Ellie. She was momentarily transported to the day her mom click-clacked into her hospital room. The day all of this started.

Minutes later she was seated at a computer terminal, the Internet up. She clicked onto one of the sites that had made her stay away from the computer for the last few days.

A news site.

Once the *Phoenix Herald* home page popped up, she clicked on a link buried low on the page:

Local Newscaster's Daughter Leaves Little Girl Brain-Dead

The words, in black and white, made her really, really regret she'd eaten anything today. She didn't cry, though. She thought she should've felt like crying.

But she didn't. She didn't feel anything. Not even the shoes pinching her toes.

Jayne concentrated on each word of the article. She hadn't known any of this. Then again, she hadn't wanted to know any of this. And her family, whether they had known about the details or not, hadn't told her about any of this.

For now, she forgot about her family and what they didn't tell her. Instead, she read about six-year-old Brenda Deavers.

About how she wasn't wearing a seat belt.

About how the air bag hit her after the head-on.

About how the impact snapped her neck.

And broke it.

10

SOMETHING WAS DIGGING into her arm. Jayne glanced down. A piece of notebook paper, folded into a triangle, was poking into her.

It was third period. Honors English Lit. It was her first class of the day. After two periods in the library, Mrs. Fullerton had prodded her to go to class. It wasn't an order, though. The librarian had helped Jayne with enough research papers to know that the sixteen-year-old was a bright, conscientious student not given to ditching class.

As such, Jayne received a polite nudge. "Jayne, why don't you get yourself to class? You wouldn't want to miss too much more school, would you?"

Jayne had taken the hint. She'd also heard the words Mrs. Fullerton had left out: *You wouldn't want to miss too much more school than you have because you broke that little girl's neck, would you?*

She'd gotten to class ten minutes after it started, holding a hall pass from Mrs. Fullerton saying she'd been "helping out" in the library. She took her seat while Mrs. Peabody lectured about *The Scarlet Letter.*

She had just started discussing Hester Prynne's public humiliation in the town square.

Jayne could relate.

Her arm was being poked again. She clenched her teeth together and took the note. She never got notes. She wasn't a note kind of girl. And Janice Wells, a quiet girl with a solid B average, was a well-known pawn in the note-passing game.

The note had to have come from the Wicked Witches in the back row.

Jayne was on the front. She didn't recognize the handwriting. There were flowers with large petals and heart centers on both sides.

The happy scrawl across the paper didn't fool her. This wasn't a note taking a poll about which guy was the hottest or asking what she was doing Friday night. She didn't get notes like that.

Which meant it was a note searching for gossip about the accident.

Jayne went with her gut. She tore the note in half and stuffed the pieces in the last pages of her book.

She didn't give a crud what was in that note. Or what people were thinking about her.

Then why did she keep thinking about how long it would take to tape that note together again?

At lunch, Jayne sneaked a diet pop into the reference section of the library. Most of the students who came to the library were there to check e-mail on the opposite side of the silent, over-air-conditioned room.

This side of the library was the perfect hideout. No one ever came to use the encyclopedias anymore. Not when there was Wikipedia.com.

"Jaynie, I think it's time you stopped ignoring me."

Jayne's hand jerked, spilling soda droplets on the table. Her heart stopped for a millisecond longer than usual, the good girl in her worrying that one of Mrs. Fullerton's assistants had caught her with the contraband drink.

But it was just Tom standing in front of her. His dark blue eyes were—what? Sad? Annoyed?

"You almost made me pee my pants, Tom. Good job." She attempted a smile, but her nerves were stretched too thin for that. She concentrated on using a piece of notebook paper to wipe up the amber spill. "How'd you find me?"

"I know your favorite study areas." He sat down and put his backpack on the table. He leaned over it, his voice low. "Hey, did you get my messages? I e-mailed you, IM'ed you. I even braved your mom and phoned you a couple of times. Well, I left messages with your dad, but still. She probably knows about them."

Jayne saw the teasing in his eyes, but she also saw some hurt. He didn't deserve her being a crappy friend. But it went hand in hand with feeling like a crappy human being.

"Life's just been a little nutty, you know?" She closed the French textbook that had been open in front of her. She hadn't been studying, anyway. "I wasn't up for chitchat."

"I know you've been through a lot. Ellie's told me most of it, and I heard a lot on the news." His hands played with a strap on his backpack, and he concentrated on the knots he was making. "I also saw the reporters out there today, stalking you." His mouth twisted in disgust. "I just wanted to let you know I'm here if you need to, you know, whatever."

Tom wasn't too good with words sometimes, but he always meant what he said. Well, at least what he *tried* to say.

"I appreciate that." She absentmindedly opened and closed the cover of the French book. Jayne wasn't going to take him up on that offer to spill her guts anytime soon. She couldn't do that with anyone. Not with her parents, not with her sister, not with Larry the Fairy, not with the media.

The little girl was brain-dead. Not just hurt, as in physical therapy hurt.

But brain-dead. Like one step away from *dead* dead.

She couldn't say those words out loud. They were ugly, ugly, soul-crunching words.

When she was going to talk, it was going to be to that lawyer. And even then, hopefully, she wouldn't have to *talk* talk. *Maybe I can just hand him Mom's notebook and let him look up the answers.*

"Hey, I brought you something." Tom pulled his hand away from his backpack and dug around in the front pocket. "It isn't really anything. Just something, you know, to make you feel a little better."

He gave her a crumpled lunch bag. Inside was a framed photo of both of them sitting on the curb outside a roadside diner. Tom's head was on her knee, and she was sticking her tongue out while she made bunny ears behind him.

"Finally." She managed a weak smile. "I've been after you forever to get this developed."

She cradled the cheap black frame as she remembered that

day on Route 66. They'd been outside of Flagstaff, on their way to the Painted Desert. Her dad had dragged her mom out to look at hieroglyphics; Jayne, Tom, and Ellie had amused themselves by taking tons of pictures. Jayne with her digital Nikon, Tom with his disposable cardboard camera.

"Ellie took this one, right?"

Tom grinned. "Yeah. The one your mom took is blocked by her thumb. For such a skinny woman, she's sure got a fat thumb."

"It's great. Thanks." She slipped the photo into her messenger bag. The moment of happiness started to give way to sadness. The picture had been taken this past March. The biggest worry she'd had back then was how to study for four tests while fitting in ten hours of tennis practice and putting on three car washes in one Saturday for three different clubs she belonged to.

The good old days.

"Jayne, are you sure you don't want to talk?" Tom attempted a wink. He wasn't very good at it, though. He never was. "This is your chance to unload on me. Ellie things. Gen things. Any things."

The first bell rang.

"Nope, I'm good."

Tom got up, his hands again twisting the backpack strap. "We better get going, then. Heard a rumor there's a pop quiz in chemistry."

A pop quiz she hadn't studied for. Yeah, that was going to get her on her feet and pushing her way through the crowds.

Jayne opened her French book again. "That's okay. You go ahead. I'll be right behind you."

She looked up when Tom didn't say anything. He had his backpack over one shoulder and was looking intently at the strap. He was contemplating something. He definitely had on his "How do I put this" face.

He'd had that same look when he told her his dog had eaten their team art project in fifth grade. That had been the first and last time Jayne had been partners with him.

She closed her book and rolled her eyes. "What? Whatever it is, just tell me."

He finally met her eyes. "I know you're trying to avoid people, but I can walk you to class. No biggie."

"Why?" A hint of suspicion was in her tone. It wasn't like she was Gloria Salas, his girlfriend in ninth grade. The one who'd led him around on a leash and had him opening doors and walking her to class and making him blow his pizza-job money on her.

"We'll be going past Jenna's and Lori's lockers."

Jayne looked down at the cover of her French book, warped after a decade of students using it. She forced out, "So?"

"So, I don't want you to have to deal with whatever Jenna's going to say to you."

Jenna? Lori was the evil one of the two. Jenna was just the bumbling sidekick. "I can deal with Jenna. You know she's just Lori's lackey."

He gave her an odd look. "Lori isn't your problem nowadays. You know that, right?"

Tom might as well have been speaking Swahili. She would've understood what he was saying just as clearly.

"I know what, Tom?"

He dropped his bag back on the table and crouched down beside her. He had that "How do I put this" look on his face again. Times one hundred.

"Jayne, the girl from the accident. Brenda Deavers?" He swallowed, his Adam's apple bobbing. "Jenna is her sister."

11

WHERE'S THAT PEARL NECKLACE I put on your dresser this morning?"

Jayne awkwardly pulled her seat belt across her body with her right arm. The purr of the Jaguar barely made a sound over the Tchaikovsky playing around her. Tchaikovsky meant her mother was trying to de-stress.

Jayne had a feeling she knew what Gen was stressed about. And it wasn't Ellie.

"I didn't see the necklace. Sorry." She had seen it, but she hated the choking feeling necklaces gave her.

Her mom's silence was louder than if she *had* said something. Gen Thompkins, the master of guilt-tripping.

"And why didn't you call me back? I left a message on your cell reminding you to bring the notebook."

Jayne tapped the book in her lap. "I have it right here."

What she didn't tell her mom was that she had turned off the cell phone right after lunch. That's when the text messages had started rolling in.

Poor little Jaynie-Waynie hiding out in the librerry. Murderurs belong in jails, not librerrys.

There were four more text messages waiting to be read after that one. She had a feeling they were from Jenna and Lori.

Not just because they were the witches of Palm Desert High. But because Jenna's sister was in a hospital because of Jayne.

If Ellie had been put in the hospital because of Jenna or Lori, who knew what kind of vindictive things Jayne might find herself doing.

After that first message, she'd deleted the rest without reading any and then turned off the phone.

She just wished she could turn off her thoughts that easily. The ones about a cold cell. And bread and water.

And roommates named Bertha.

The car rolled away from the curb and maneuvered through after-school pickup traffic. It had been forever and a day since Jayne had been picked up by a parent. She'd been taking the bus since she'd been big enough to carry a bus pass and not lose it. When she'd finally gotten her license in February, she'd been glad to get away from the bus smells and random bus fights.

Her license. She hadn't thought about that. Like it mattered. Her car was in the shop, anyway. "Do you think my license will be suspended?"

"Probably." Her mom almost sounded as if she didn't care. And a little put out, as if she knew she'd have to pick Jayne up more often. "Some judges suspend it until you're eighteen, others until you're twenty-one. There was one case Diane Googled where a boy had his suspended until he was thirty.

For a second, Jayne panicked at the thought of not having a car for fourteen years. Just as quickly, she felt guilty for having that thought. That little girl was never going to learn to drive.

Uh-oh. Tears were stinging her eyes. Time for a new thought. Math. Math was good.

If it's two and a half miles from home to school, all relatively flat, and I want to get to school in ten minutes, I'd have to do a four-minute mile, which is fifteen miles per hour. Okay, not possible. How about twenty minutes...

Of course, she had to get a bike first. She'd have to look up which ones were the best. That made her realize what else her mom had said. "You had Diane look up what I could be punished with?"

Her mom didn't take her eyes off the road as she reapplied her nude lipstick. At least one Thompkins didn't take her eyes off the road. "I certainly don't have time to do the research."

Jayne stared at the after-school traffic ahead of them, which made them stop and start every few seconds. She consciously unclenched her hands. She needed to stay focused on the lawyer stuff. Getting mad at her mom was a daily occurrence, but she'd learned by now that calling her mom out on her bad behavior was never a good idea. Knowing Gen, she'd pull the car over and make Jayne walk to the lawyer to show her what a bad mom looked like.

She'd done it before. She'd definitely do it again.

Jayne closed her eyes briefly and tried to calm her nerves. She had a good impression to make, especially since this lawyer guy was going to have her future in his hands.

"Have you talked to him already? The lawyer, I mean."

"Briefly. And it's a her." Her mom switched lanes and turned down the CD. "There wasn't too much to talk about. We won't know much about what's going to happen until after we talk to the police."

She slammed her palm on the horn as a guy stopped too fast in front of them. "They've already cited you for running a red light. They had witnesses for that. We just need to know what the court systems are going to do with you."

What the court systems are going to do with me. Jayne looked down at her feet and clicked the pointy toes of her ugly black pumps together. She did some breathing exercises her dad had taught her to do right before a test.

"You can even do these exercises when you're taking those tests at Harvard, where they last for three days and make you act out the essay questions," he'd teased.

Like you have a chance at going to Harvard, a small voice scoffed in the back of her head. Jayne concentrated on her breathing again. With each breath in and out, she repeated: *Re-lax. Re-lax. Har-vard. Go-ing. No-where.*

The Senior Student award, on the other hand . . . that was a moot point. With all the media coverage she'd been getting, the selection committee had probably dumped her application in the trash.

She raised her arms away from her body a little to dry out the sweat under her armpits.

The lawyer's office was on the tenth floor of a high-rise in downtown Phoenix and had a reception area that looked like an advertisement for fake plants. Plastic ficuses and philodendrons were everywhere, even in plant holders above each window.

Before Jayne could really analyze the kind of person who put fake plants in natural sunlight, the receptionist told her she could go right in.

It took a few steps before she realized her mom wasn't right behind her. In fact, her mom was sitting by a plastic fern, checking messages on her handheld.

"Mom?"

"Go on ahead. I'll be there in a sec."

Her mom sat there as calm as could be, typing into her Black-Berry. Not breathing down Jayne's neck. Was this some sort of test? There was one way to find out. In an antagonistic voice that usually pissed her mom off, she asked, "But don't you want to make sure I say the right thing?"

Gen looked up briefly, a tight smile on her lips. "I have faith in you." Looking back down, she added, "That's why you have that notebook of questions and answers I edited."

The lawyer's office was small and wood-paneled with a tinier, more condensed jungle. A red-haired woman with fuchsia nails and albino skin rose from behind a huge mahogany desk. She took one of Jayne's hands in both of hers.

The grip felt cool and strong.

"Jayne, right?" The woman stood about four inches shorter than her, even with three-inch purple heels. "I'm Valerie Shet-land. Call me Val. Please, have a seat. The officer who was at the scene of the accident will be here in a few minutes, after we've had a chance to talk for a bit."

She smelled like sandalwood and lavender. The smell seemed ... confident.

Val walked around her desk, her strides long and sure-footed. "Sit, sit. I've asked your mom to wait outside while we get acquainted for a minute."

Jayne thought it had been weird when her mom hung back. Doubly weird when she said she trusted Jayne to handle herself. Gen Thompkins always wanted to be in the thick of things. In the thick of Jayne's life.

Val must've read Jayne's thoughts on her face, because she laughed. "Yeah, it was like pulling teeth to have her wait out there. But she respects my decisions. Including the one that will have her finding other representation if she doesn't like those decisions."

Jayne sat stiffly on the edge of a chair that was overshadowed by a huge flowering plant. Fake, of course. It looked like that human-eating plant in that movie *Little Shop of Horrors* she'd seen with Ellie a couple of years ago during their campy horror-film phase. She started feeling claustrophobic and had to remember those breathing exercises again. She rearranged one of the fronds pushing against her shoulder.

"Sorry about that. I just love plants to death. They're my Zen. The woman who comes to dust them every week must've moved that one." She added in a loud whisper, "I kill the real ones in five days or less, so I got these fake ones and treat them like they're real. Weird, huh?"

Yeah. "No, not really."

Val smiled, like she knew she was being humored. "Your mom tells me you both went over the accident already?"

Jayne nodded mutely.

"Great. Figuring out the exact details of that day will help us build a rock-solid case."

"Case?" Jayne's voice raised a few octaves. She remembered the notebook she was holding. She held it out in Val's direction. "Mom and I went over stuff you might want to know. Here are the answers."

Val laughed and took the notebook. She started flipping through the pages as she walked around the desk. "Are you going to be a journalist like your mom?"

"No." The answer came fast and furious. Which was unexpected. Jayne had never really given much thought to being a journalist. That her subconscious already knew the answer before she did . . . that was interesting.

What else did her subconscious know that she didn't?

Val continued to scan the notebook. "The juvenile court system will want to try you for assault with a deadly weapon, what with that little girl still in her brain-dead state." She started making notes on a yellow legal pad. "It's a manslaughter charge. And because you weren't drinking or on drugs—that I know of and that we'll get to in a minute—that's a misdemeanor. Which basically means no jail time and you can still vote when you turn eighteen."

A cloud of spiderwebs had taken up residence in Jayne's head. "It's only a misdemeanor?"

"Yep. As long as you didn't have any mind-altering substances in your system or weren't going a criminally negligent speed"—Val flipped through some notes on her desk—"which, according to the tire marks you made with your car, you weren't. The police report states you may have been going five, six miles over the speed limit. That still clears you for a misdemeanor."

Jayne stared blankly at the large turquoise pendant Val was

wearing. It was freaky that people who hadn't even been in the car with her could figure out how fast she'd been going.

"Then there's the civil suit if the family wants punitive damages, which I think they will. America's too sue-happy a place for the Deavers family *not* to take you to civil court. And with all the news coverage this story's gotten, the people in the red"—she glanced at her notes again—"Toyota and black Mercedes definitely know your family's got money."

Val picked up the papers, tapped them on the desk to straighten out the edges, and returned them to the folder, which she snapped shut. "Even with this dandy notebook you've given me, it's time for me to ask you a few questions. Up for it, Jayne?"

Jayne nodded numbly, still mesmerized by Val's pendant and the fact that all of this was a misdemeanor.

That maybe she still had a chance at Harvard. But did she deserve to go to Harvard?

"Based on the toxicology reports from the hospital, you had no drugs or alcohol in your system. So that's good." She flipped open the notebook. "Was there anything else distracting you that day?"

Jayne thought back to the notebook with Gen's red-ink edits. "Nothing more than the usual distractions."

Val laughed. "Spoken like someone whose mom does incriminating interviews for a living. But I'm not the cops. *Was* there anything distracting you? Just in case there are witnesses that will report otherwise."

Witnesses. The guy in the Diamondbacks hat. The voice coming from the area by her feet. "I was answering my cell phone."

Val wrote it on the yellow pad of paper. "That's not an offense in Arizona. Even if it was, you'd still be in misdemeanor territory."

The way Val kept throwing "misdemeanor" around, like what had happened was no big deal, made Jayne feel better and worse at the same time. Better because she felt like maybe she could still have a future.

Worse because being charged with a misdemeanor didn't seem right for making someone brain-dead.

Her left leg started jiggling, and if Tom had been around, he'd tell her she was driving him nuts.

The phone on Val's desk buzzed. Depressing a button, the woman barked, "Yes?"

"Police Officer Bradley is here, Ms. Shetland."

"Great. Send him and Mrs. Thompkins in."

Jayne breathed. In-two-three-out-two-three-four-five. It didn't help. She still wanted to run as fast as these stupid heels would let her. Her cool, white, down-comforted bed would be perfect.

A familiar-looking man opened the door. He was the officer who'd given her the thumbs-up sign at the accident. He stepped aside to let her mom in first.

"Officer Bradley?" Val greeted him with a handshake and a gesture to take a seat. "We spoke on the phone already."

Val ignored Jayne's mom. Seeing this, Jayne felt oddly better. It was nice that for once her mom wasn't the center of attention and that the woman representing Jayne's future in a court of law wasn't wasting her time brownnosing Gen Thompkins like half of the Phoenix population did.

"Jayne, I'm here to make sure that the officer doesn't tread on any of your rights while we discuss the day the accident occurred. I will speak on your behalf if he asks a question that I do not want you to respond to, okay?"

Jayne nodded. Her throat felt like she'd just run a half-marathon without any water. Val poured her a glass of water without saying anything and briefly squeezed the shoulder of her good arm before retreating behind the desk again.

"Miss Thompkins." Officer Bradley flipped to a page in his notebook while Jayne sat with her clasped hands squeezed between her thighs. She now knew what it felt like to feel as close to throwing up without *actually* throwing up. "Today is your only meeting with me. Next week, they'll probably get you on the juvie court docket where you'll appear in front of a judge who'll give you a court date and a probation officer."

"Probation officer?" Jayne felt her mouth go dry. She'd only heard about hardened criminals having probation officers. Guys with tattoos and crusty apartments and really bad drug habits.

"Yes." He looked down at whatever was written in his note-pad. His bald head was red from too much sun and not enough sunscreen. "Until this goes to court, you'll need to check in with her every day. You'll also be released to your parents, which means you need to always tell them your whereabouts."

"Released to my parents?" Not that it mattered. She was home 24/7 anyway.

"Until this case goes to court. You will also not be able to drive, given the situation . . ."

Jayne had started tuning him out. She twisted her gold watch around on her wrist, barely aware of what she was doing. She sneaked a quick glance at her mom, but Gen was concentrating on whatever Officer Bradley was saying.

She tuned back into the conversation when she heard the man clear his throat. The faint smell of a sweet cigarette was coming off of him. Cloves, maybe? Her grams smoked those. "We'll start off slow and simple. Ready?"

Jayne nodded.

"One, you had a red light when you hit the red Toyota."

Jayne nodded.

"The tox reports from the hospital show you had no drugs or alcohol in your system. That's good. Now, were you—" The chirp of a high-pitched ring tone interrupted his words. He pulled a cell phone from his belt. "Excuse me."

Jayne tried to calm her nerves while he talked. *No big deal. Breathe. He just wants the facts about that day. You don't have anything to hide. So what if you're confined to school and home? You do that anyway. And the car thing? You knew that already. And there's no way you were going to touch the Jetta again, anyway.*

Officer Bradley was still on the phone. Jayne didn't turn to look at her mom to judge her reaction to all of this. Right now, Val and her note-taking was making her feel better. She was just glad her dad wasn't here. He was home with Ellie, working on his notes for some all-natural product line he was developing for some big cosmetic company.

She'd also asked him to stay home.

If he had been here, he'd be holding her hand and trying to

shelter her from the harsher things the lawyer wanted to say. She didn't need that. It was time to face the truth. The truth would be nice for once.

That way she wouldn't be blindsided by a woman with a mike and a fake concerned look on her face.

Jayne chewed on her lip, eating the little bit of lip gloss that was still on.

The officer clicked his phone shut and made a phlegm-filled sniff as he reattached it to his belt. "That was my captain." He looked at Jayne, and her heart sank even before he said the words. "Brenda Deavers was taken off life support an hour ago. She's dead."

TWO MONTHS LATER . . .

12

WILL THE DEFENDANT PLEASE RISE."

Jayne felt weak. Val stood next to her, holding her hand. It would've been too awkward with their height differences to try to put an arm around Jayne's shoulders.

Val was so tiny, Jayne felt like she was the one offering her hand for comfort. Then again, she wasn't her usual Amazon self lately. She felt like she'd shrunk an inch or two, and based on the waist of the skirt she was wearing, she'd lost an inch or two around her waist.

"Jayne Lee Thompkins, you have pled guilty to vehicular manslaughter. Do you wish to say anything before sentencing is imposed?"

Jayne's mouth felt like she'd licked chalk dust from a blackboard. There'd been no testimony, just Jayne meeting with Val and the prosecutor to go over the accident and work out what her punishment would be.

And she was numb.

Over the last eight weeks, Jayne had been numb. And she was sort of glad about that.

Especially when she'd gone to her locker and a new, horrible name had been written in permanent marker. Daily. Sometimes even twice a day.

She'd gotten a new phone, but someone figured out her number and the text messaging started again. Finally, she just stopped turning her phone on. And taking it with her.

Her house had been egged. Three times. The last time, a bag of dog crap had been thrown at her front door. Her mom had gotten the police out to the house to test for fingerprints.

Like high school students would have their fingerprints on file. Or at least not the two in particular who Jayne knew had vandalized her locker. Stalked her phone. Egged the house. Desecrated her front door.

Jenna and Lori.

They'd been writing daily blogs about "Child Killer Thompkins." They'd scanned Jayne's yearbook picture and used Photoshop to put her in an electric chair, her brain sizzling and tiny lightning bolts coming off her body.

Jayne hadn't seen it. Tammy, Ellie's mall buddy, had told her one day around a mouth full of s'mores while standing in the Thompkinses' kitchen.

Jenna was here today, sitting by her mom. They were behind the guy from the state, the one prosecuting Jayne. Mrs. Deavers's eyes were vacant, a crumpled tissue in her hand. Jenna looked at the ground, her arms crossed.

Neither had looked at Jayne once.

Val had told her Mrs. Deavers would be here today. Family members usually were, in order to have input on sentencing.

Sentencing. That's why they were here. To determine her future. Or lack of one.

She closed her eyes for a moment. She wanted to sleep through the rest of high school. She sort of already had. She'd left half her finals blank, and the other half she had to guess at. She hadn't done any studying since . . . since the day in Val's office. When she'd found out Brenda Deavers had been taken off life support and had her organs harvested.

She'd tried to study. For two months, she'd sit at her desk and open her books. Turn on her computer. But then images of the accident and the little girl would freeze her brain and make her useless for the rest of the day. She'd turn on crap TV and watch reruns of shows she hadn't even liked when they were first on.

She had no idea what her grades were. Usually she kept a piece of paper in her notebook with each and every grade recorded. Not this quarter.

There hadn't been too many good grades to record.

She was halfway hoping her teachers would give her A's by default. For just being Jayne Thompkins. If they didn't . . . the crap was really going to hit the fan.

College applications would be the least of her worries. First, she'd have to keep Gen from killing her.

Val squeezed her hand and Jayne shook herself out of her thoughts. The judge needed an answer. What had been the question? *Do you wish to say anything before sentencing is imposed?* Val and her mom had coached her last night for a good two hours about what she needed to say right now.

She licked her lips and started to speak, her voice thready and quiet at first before growing more solid and normal-sounding. "I wish to apologize to the Deavers family. I can never take back that day, that horrible Tuesday. I wish I could go back, more than words can say, and change the events of that day. But I can't, and I'm sorry."

Jayne dropped her eyes down to the legal pad she'd been doodling on for the last hour. She couldn't look in the judge's watery blue eyes anymore. She just wanted this over with.

"I understand the Deavers family is in this courtroom today," the judge said. "Would a representative of the family like to say anything?"

Jayne tried to keep from looking around. But the silence, the waiting, seemed to drone on. She slowly turned her head so she could see what the Deaverses were doing.

Jenna and her mom stayed seated, neither looking like they had moved an inch. Finally, Mrs. Deavers shook her head and raised the wadded tissue to her nose, sniffing into it.

Jayne bit the inside of her lip. This was it. This was where the judge told her she'd be the first person to ever get the death penalty for a misdemeanor.

It could happen. Val could've missed a loophole.

"Based on the plea agreement reached between the state and the defendant, Jayne Lee Thompkins has been found delinquent on the charge of vehicular manslaughter. I hereby sentence her to community service not to exceed one thousand hours and to be completed within the next 365 days. I also hereby suspend Jayne Lee Thompkins's license, not to be reinstated until her eighteenth birthday. On the successful completion of said community service, the record of this event will be sealed." She heard him shuffling papers. "You are also mandated to fifty hours of counseling, to be completed within the time frame of your community service."

Jayne kept her eyes fixated on the cheap laminate desk she stood over. She waited to hear the words *We've changed our mind, Jayne Lee Thompkins. You'll be going to jail for the rest of your natural born life. Your roommate's name is Bertha. You two will grow quite close, I assure you.*

She waited.

"Miss Thompkins."

Her stomach lurched. Here it was. She raised her eyes to the judge.

"I want you to take this opportunity to really reflect on where you want your life to go. This is a misdemeanor, meaning that you will not have to check the felony box on any college or job applications. I know that your life prior to this event had you on track for a bright, promising future. I do not want you to lose sight of that future, Miss Thompkins."

He shuffled his papers around. Jayne kept waiting for him to say that prison would be just the thing to keep her focused on her future.

"Based on this, I want you to fulfill your community service at Outreach Arizona. This program focuses on helping teenagers who don't have a wonderful future. They may have a mother or father in prison; they may be facing pregnancy while trying to finish school. I think this will be a good opportunity for you to see people who think all is lost. Maybe how you're feeling right at this moment."

He looked around. Jayne knew this was it. This was when she

was going to get her real punishment. She was getting off too easy after killing a child.

Wasn't she?

Instead, he said, "I want you to check back with me in six months' time, to see how you are." He banged his gavel. "Court is dismissed."

"It could've gone a lot worse, Jayne." Val, Jayne, and Jayne's parents stood in the orange-carpeted foyer of the juvenile court building. Val's voice was uncharacteristically low as she said, "All this may seem overwhelming right now, but it was a fair sentence. Do you have any questions about it?"

Jayne shook her head, her blonde ponytail feeling like a million pounds. She took out the elastic band.

"How long is this community service lasting again?" her mom demanded, pushing a stray piece of hair behind her ear and smiling at a few passing lawyers who were trying to act cool at seeing a local celeb. There was always someone who recognized Gen Thompkins. Be it the restroom at the movie theater or the court at her daughter's manslaughter hearing. "I want to make sure I program it into the BlackBerry."

Val put an arm around Jayne's back. "A year. That's about four hours a day, five days a week." She turned and squeezed Jayne against her side. "For a girl like you, this will be a walk in the park. Just treat it like one of those extracurriculars you have."

Jayne remained silent. The extracurriculars she *used* to have. Before she quit them all—Key Club, the school paper, French Club—to stay in her room when she wasn't at school.

"Outreach Arizona's a good place." Her dad squeezed her shoulder, before his hand awkwardly fell back to his side. "It's only a few miles from home."

"And it will look good on the college résumé," her mother interjected, slipping the handheld into her purse. She was standing about ten feet away from them. Gen had to get back to editing a story about six-year-old beauty queens, and Jayne was only too happy to be Gen-free. "You don't have to mention it was community service."

Jayne nodded, not saying anything. There wasn't anything to say.

The judge had sentenced her, the case had been shut, and her mother had found the silver lining in killing a kid.

"I was thinking we could go see Larry next week."

Her dad maneuvered the Prius through Friday rush hour. Larry. Larry? Uh-oh. *Larry*. As in fairy. She concentrated on the brake lights of the car ahead of them and didn't say anything, hoping he'd take the hint and drop the topic.

Jayne scraped the edge of the card Val had given her along her skirt, thinking back to her parting words.

"We still don't know if there's going to be a civil case." Val had said. "We usually hear about one after the judge comes back with a verdict. Especially a verdict that isn't liked. Think O.J., Robert Blake. They got off but the families of the deceased were still able to nail them."

Jayne knew Val wasn't too good with censoring her thoughts. But O.J.? Robert Blake?

She was just a misdemeanor-er. Whatever that meant.

Val pulled Jayne aside when they got to the parking garage and her dad was already in the car. "If you ever need me, babe, I'm a phone call, e-mail, or fax away. You're going to have it pretty rough these next couple of months. Good kids like you usually do."

In a lower voice, she'd added, "Your dad seems pretty approachable, but he seems like he's in la-la land. Typical parent response after an accident like this. Give him time to pull it together, okay?"

Val didn't bring up Gen as someone to talk to.

"I think seeing him will help, Jaynie." Her dad's voice brought her out of her thoughts. What was he talking about? Oh, yeah. Larry the Fairy. "Plus, he'll help with those fifty hours of counseling the judge wants." He pulled into the left lane. "Talking to a family friend might be easier than talking to some stranger."

Jayne tightened her arms over her chest, warding off the chill she was starting to feel from the air conditioner blasting on her. She didn't want to share *anything* with Larry. Feelings or astrological signs or who needs to be kicked off *American Idol*.

"It's okay, kiddo. You don't have to answer now. I just wanted to put Larry out there again." He briefly touched her leg with the back of his fingers. "If you want, me and your mom can go with you to see Larry. We can have a family therapy session of sorts."

"No!" Jayne didn't even know she was going to say the word before it was blurted out.

The Thompkins family talking about Jayne's biggest mistake with Larry as an audience member? Her dad might as well have suggested stripping naked in front of Jenna and Lori and letting them circle her fat with permanent marker and writing "Killer" on her forehead.

It was almost the same thing.

13

THE OLD STUCCO BUILDING looked like it had once been a church. Seeing it, Jayne wondered why such a big building was necessary for talking to a bunch of kids about how to juggle a baby and classes.

"Are you sure this is where you're supposed to be, Jayne?" Her dad leaned against the steering wheel, looking around the deserted parking lot. "I would've thought there'd be more cars."

"Everyone's parked in the back." Jayne put her water bottle in her bag as she opened the door. "Maria told me to park back there if I had a car."

If this Maria chick had half a brain, she would've known Jayne couldn't drive and that she was coming to this godforsaken place because some idiot DMV person let her get behind the wheel in the first place.

She got out and looked around. They were in an older part of Paradise Valley, where horse trails ran alongside the concrete sidewalks. A hitching post stood next to the bus stop.

"You have everything?"

"Yep." She kept the sigh she wanted to expel to herself. In the week since the judge had sentenced her, her dad had been like a friggin' puppy. Everywhere she turned, he'd been there, wanting to give her hugs and long, sad stares.

Classic Dad. He almost made up for the other parental unit.

"Money?"

Jayne nodded. She wanted to get the day started. The sooner she signed in, the sooner the next four hours would be over. Then she could go back to her room and the pj's she'd left on top of her bed.

"Just so you know, I'm aware of the surprise party tonight."

Jayne looked at her watch. She had two minutes to get in there and report for her first day of penance. "What surprise party?"

"It's okay, honey." He chuckled. "Ellie caved and told me last week." At her blank stare, he added, "About the surprise party your mother planned for my forty-fifth?"

That's right.

The subject of the conversation she'd had with her mom right before she crashed. She'd never ended up calling Grams about the party. Her mom must've talked Ellie into playing the middleman.

Jayne wondered briefly if her mom had given Ellie the duty on the same day as the accident. Or if she'd waited until the next day.

"Anyway, I'll be here at around five-thirty so we can go out to Sun City to pick up Grams and take her to the 'quiet dinner' your mom has planned." He air-quoted his words, and Jayne tried to muster a smile. It was hard to get excited over a birthday when it was hard enough just to get out of bed.

She waved good-bye and slammed the door shut. Jayne started dragging herself up the sidewalk, one foot in front of the other, when her dad called out, "You're sure you're good?"

Good? That was an overstatement. Surviving, yeah. She turned around and gave a tired little smile. "I'm fine, Dad. Go home. Go pull those weeds you're always complaining about."

Inside the black double doors, a front desk took up a third of the reception area. A pixielike girl with short, spiky black hair sat behind it. "You here for abstinence counseling?"

As the girl turned to look at the clock behind her, Jayne saw a Chinese symbol tattooed on the back of her neck in red ink.

"Go on back. You've got five minutes till they start."

"No thanks." Jayne cleared her throat and tightened her hold on the strap of her bag. "I mean, I'm not here for that. I'm here to see Maria? About starting today?"

The girl looked her up and down as if she was taking the measure of her. "I would've pegged you as a save-yourself-for-marriage sort. The ponytail and the clothes fooled me."

They walked through a large room, about the size of Palm Desert High's library. Cubicles partitioned the room, and one side was taken up with a mishmash of what looked like third-hand furniture: a plaid couch, a couple of vinyl beanbag chairs, a klatch of straight-backed chairs in gray nubby material.

Tattoo Girl also had tribal tattoos inked in rings around her right upper arm and left calf. Jayne became mesmerized by the one on her calf as they walked the mile to the back of the building. She wondered if that tattoo had hurt the most. Or how Tattoo Girl would hide it once she got a real job and was a slave to pantyhose and skirts.

Also, what kind of parent would let their seventeen-, eighteen-year-old kid get a tattoo? If Jayne ever got a tattoo, her mom would hurt her more than any needle would.

At the back of the building, they stopped at an office with a window that let everyone look inside and whoever was inside keep an eye on the outside. A brunette in her thirties was talking on the phone while she painted her big toenail a chromelike blue. She wiped at the corner of a toe with her thumb. Jayne wondered what she was going to do with the paint smear that was now on her skin. She got her answer when the woman wiped it under her desk.

"I'm definitely on the same page you are, Ken. Remember, we wrote the book together. But I have to stand firm on this. As a nonprofit, I have to watch our pennies. And everything for that night has already been paid for. Nonrefundable paid."

She tilted her head to the side, saw the girls in the doorway, and motioned them in. Tattoo Girl made herself comfortable on the tapestry love seat and picked up a crumpled magazine. Since she took up the entire length of the sofa, Jayne had no other option than to maneuver herself awkwardly onto a denim beanbag in the corner.

"Great, Ken. I knew we could come to a solution together. Yeah, send me an e-mail confirming everything. Bye." She hung up and screwed down the cap of the nail polish. "Ryan, remind me again why I do this job?"

"Because the pay keeps you in that bling bling you like so much." The girl on the couch didn't look up from her *Newsweek*.

"Oh, yeah. Thanks for the reality check." The woman turned

to Jayne and scooted forward on the wheeled chair with the heels of her feet. Feet that were bare and had black soles from what looked to be the less-than-clean industrial carpet. "You must be Jayne. I'm Maria."

Jayne pushed herself up to shake her extended hand. She let go when her stomach muscles couldn't hold her in the weird scrunched-over position any longer.

"I hear we have you for a year. Is that right?"

Jayne nodded numbly. A year. It sounded so permanent.

"Great. Ryan, show her where to put her bag and where the lunchroom and bathrooms are. Then bring her back to me and we'll get you up to speed on your daily duties, okay?" Maria's brown eyes crinkled at the corners as she directed this last part at Jayne. She picked up the nail polish. "Plus, that should give me enough time to do the other foot."

Ryan showed Jayne the lockers where she could lock up her stuff. Rather, she half-lifted an arm in the direction of the lockers and sighed, "Your crap goes there."

Jayne pulled out a sweatshirt before she put the bag in the locker and turned the key. "Is it always this cold in here?"

"Right as rain, princess."

Princess? She didn't deserve that. She had on Old Navy jeans. Rhinestone flip-flops. A gold Bulova watch.

"I'm not a princess." Hearing herself say the words, even she wasn't convinced.

"Is Harvard paying for itself, then?"

Jayne looked down again. She was holding a crimson sweatshirt, the Harvard crest in full view. She didn't know why she'd brought it. She didn't really want to think about it.

"This was a gift." From her mother, with the words "Make me proud" attached. "It doesn't mean anything."

Her voice cracked saying the words.

Ryan raised an eyebrow. The unpierced one. The smaller girl didn't say anything else as she finished up the tour filled with lots of pointing. Point left: break room. Point in two of the four corners of the building: restrooms. There were about twenty people filling up half of the cubicles, most in their late teens.

"Is Maria the only adult here?" Jayne stared at the back of her guide. Her skirt looked like it was Goodwill and had a tear running almost to her butt. It worked, though. It went with her black Doc Martens, black tights, and spiked dog collar.

Ryan let out something that sounded like a snort. "Define 'adult.'"

"Can legally drink. Has a lower insurance rate than the rest of us."

"Within the confines of those definitions, yeah, sure."

"Hey sunshine!" A guy with a "Saguaro High Basketball" shirt sat on one of the chairs in the sitting area Jayne had passed earlier. A girl with a short blonde shag sat next to him crunching through a bag of Doritos.

"I'm not in the mood, dipwad." Ryan stopped. "I assume you went out of the way to say hi because you're wanting me to introduce our new meat?"

Ryan kicked the boy's legs out of the way and started picking up some empty soda cans littering the coffee tables. "Darian Green. Meadow Haraway. This is . . . what's your name again, princess?"

"Jayne Thompkins." Jayne wanted to say, *It's Jayne Thompkins, Goth Girl Loser*. But she didn't.

That didn't stop the words from burning in her throat, though.

"So, Miss Jayne Thompkins, why are you here?" Darian crunched into an orange chip as he leaned behind Meadow. The girl seemed to be staring a little too hard at Jayne. Like she was trying to place her from somewhere. "College résumé?"

"Something like that." She crossed her arms and shivered. It really was cold in here. She'd have to bring another sweatshirt next time. Just not her Harvard one. "How about you guys?"

"Got caught selling my brother's Ritalin for recreational purposes." Meadow fiddled with the clasp on her silver link bracelet, a shiny silver heart dangling from it. "I've got another three months to work it off."

Jayne didn't know what to say to that. *Sorry you're a drug dealer* didn't seem right. Instead, she smiled and nodded in consolation.

"Don't judge us based on Meadow's lack of judgment here." Darian smiled. He looked like a guy who was used to getting people to like him. "Me? I'm in your boat. Gotta pump up my résumé in case that basketball scholarship doesn't come through."

Jayne saw Meadow raise her eyebrows as she kept searching through the chip bag. Ryan started to cough, but it was more theatrical than real.

Darian wasn't telling the truth. She got it. She stole a glance at Darian again. He was cute in a tall jock sort of way. What'd he do, get caught with alcohol in his locker, or a joint?

"Hey, princess, Maria's waiting for you." Ryan materialized by her elbow, the armful of cans gone. Jayne felt her cheeks grow warm when she heard that stupid nickname again.

Was she blushing? Wow. She was embarrassed about the nickname. And since she didn't care what Meadow thought, she must've been caring about what Darian thought.

Never in her life had she cared what a boy thought. Well, a *boy* boy. Tom didn't count.

Darian's voice followed her as she walked away. "If you get bored, my screen name is IHeartBB. It's totally gay, but Meadow picked it out."

Jayne didn't turn around. She felt weird having a boy yell to her to call him. Or rather, "IM" him. She'd never really had a guy do that before. Sure, there was Tom, but he wasn't a *guy* guy.

As they walked away, Jayne asked in a low voice, "Why is he here? Drugs?"

"Drugs?" Ryan laughed. "Sure, why not."

14

jaynie, you in there?"

Ellie's voice sounded halfway hopeful on the other side of the bedroom door. Which was weird since Jayne had stayed pretty much to herself these last couple of months and hadn't exactly been chatty. She'd become an expert at avoiding Ellie all day and night. Luckily, if she pissed off Ellie early enough, her sister would hold a grudge for a day, maybe two.

And leave her alone for a day, maybe two.

Her living her hermit life. Ellie living her life. Where the biggest worry her sister had to deal with was "Does this shirt match these shoes?"

"I'm busy." She pulled her comforter up to her chin and turned up the volume of *Three's Company*. Bad eighties TV was all she needed right now.

Mind-numbing TV after the mind-numbing day she'd just had at the Outreach place. Learning the phone system. Being given a manual about how to talk on the phone to teenagers in crisis.

Playing solitaire on the computer when Maria left her alone.

Ellie opened the door to the dark room and took in the flashing lights coming from the set. "Yeah, I can see that."

"What do you want?" Jayne didn't take her eyes off Jack and Janet trying to explain to Chrissy how to make toast.

She felt something fall onto the blanket covering her legs. "I saw this in the mail. Thought you'd want to see it before Mom and Dad."

Ellie was already at the door by the time Jayne picked up the white envelope. She saw the green palm tree in the upper left-hand corner and knew exactly what it was.

Crap. D-day had arrived.

"Don't know why I bothered. It's not like you're watching my back or anything nowadays."

Ellie mini-slammed the door before Jayne could say what was in her thoughts but what hadn't quite made it to her mouth. *I haven't watched your back, you ingrate? I'd like to see where you'd be without me. Pregnant and full of STDs, that's where you'd be!*

Whoa, where'd that come from? She didn't hate Ellie. She just . . . she just couldn't be in the same room with her right now.

Jayne glanced at the white envelope addressed "To the parents of Jayne Thompkins." It was now or never.

Before she could talk herself out of it (it being a federal felony to open someone else's mail and all), she tore open the envelope with more force than she'd intended, ripping part of the carbon copy inside.

Four C's. Two B's. A 2.3 GPA. She checked the name at the top. Maybe it was Ellie's report card. Nope. Jayne felt like a massive hand was strangling her windpipe.

Four C's. And two B's.

Before that Tuesday, she'd had over a one hundred percent in all of her classes. But then again, it had only been a couple of weeks into the fourth quarter.

The room around her blurred as her chest began to burn and tears raced down her face. Then she did the only thing she could think of. She started tearing up the report card into smaller and smaller pieces until it looked like confetti. Even then, she tried to tear the pieces some more.

But she knew it wasn't that simple. The grades were still out there, in some computer system, in some permanent record. For a nanosecond, she entertained the idea of getting someone to hack into the high school computer system.

Yeah, Jayne, then you can have a real felony on your record.

She picked up the shredded paper from her down comforter. Her mind wandered back to the last time she'd gotten her report card. She'd been ecstatic and had put it on her bulletin board along with every single report card she'd ever gotten.

Ellie called the board her A-hole Award Board. Jayne hadn't cared. It made her feel good to lie in bed and stare at the board and think about her future.

But now? What was the future? What in the hell did four C's and two B's get you? A job at Mickey D's scrubbing toilets?

She cupped the pile of paper between both her hands and dragged herself into her connecting bathroom, the muted cream color doing nothing to calm her nerves. She dumped everything into the blue water of the toilet and flushed.

Two flushes later, the four C's and two B's were gone. At least, the evidence was.

15

HOW'S IT GOING with the community service, Jaynie? Met any delinquents yet?" Grams lit up another Djarum clove cigarette. She hacked up a lung with the first puff.

Her grandmother floated on a raft a few feet from her, her one-piece showing leathery arms and legs, thin with old age. Her stomach, on the other hand, had seventy-two years' worth of pies, red meat, and ice cream puffing it up.

Jayne stared at the community swimming pool and tried not to breathe in the smoke. "Yeah, I've met a couple."

"They trying to hook you up with any doobies yet?"

Jayne hid her smile in her shirt. Her grams said whatever the heck was on her mind. It was part of the package with her. "I'm not that kinda girl, Grams. Anyway, I mainly just sit around doing nothing but answering the phone for Maria, who runs the center."

The Sun Valley Retirement Village might've been low on most teenagers' lists of places to be on a summer afternoon, but Jayne was just glad she was here and not in that cold warehouse Outreach Arizona called home. It'd been only a week since she'd started there, but it was already at the bottom of her list of "all-time greatest experiences."

"Made any friends yet?" Grams took a drink from the Bloody Mary she kept in the raft's cup holder, the clove cigarette dangling from the corner of her mouth.

Before Jayne could say anything, Ellie called over from the shallow end's steps, "You've gotta be kidding, Grams. Jayne doesn't believe in friends. She's into staying in her room all day watching crap TV."

Jayne looked up at the cloudless blue sky, trying to get the kink out of her neck. Ellie had been getting pissier and pissier with her lately. Fine by her. That meant Ellie didn't bother her.

For her insulin shots.

For homework.

For a movie.

The movie stuff, though, Jayne kind of missed. She just wasn't ready. Ready for what, she didn't know. Being normal?

Scratch that. *Feeling* normal?

Scratch that. Going back to her normal self as Ellie's go-to girl?

Yeah. Maybe.

Ellie shrieking into her cell phone interrupted her thoughts. "You were supposed to call me two hours ago, you dork!"

Jayne squeezed her eyes shut and tried to block out the sound. This was the fifth call Ellie had gotten since they'd been there. She felt pain pierce her gut.

Sure looked like Ellie was getting along just fine without her. And based on how much she was going out lately, Ellie didn't seem to be working on that FIT scholarship. Then again, Ellie never seemed to think about her future unless Jayne was pushing her.

Grams lowered her hot pink sunglasses and winked a cloudy blue eye at her. "Don't you worry none about the friend thing, Jaynie. I didn't have many friends as a girl, either."

She started to cough and took a sip of her drink. Grams had been diagnosed with emphysema a couple of years ago, but that hadn't made her cut back on anything—food, alcohol, or cigarettes. "There aren't that many quality teenagers nowadays." She sucked on her cigarette for a good five seconds and went on. "You gotta wait until you're thirty or so until you meet a divorce attorney or orthopedic surgeon at some cocktail party or PTA meeting. Now *those* are the kind of people you want to be friendly with."

Jayne smiled. Grams had been married three times and had been in and out of hospitals the last couple of years due to broken hips and wrists. Those "friends" of hers must've been why she was always getting the best divorce settlements and had the newest, best technology holding her bones and joints together.

A high-pitched giggle interrupted their conversation. Jayne wondered if Ellie was chatting up the statutory rapist she'd pulled off of her. Danny? Denny? Whoever. Whatever, it didn't matter. Her sister was a big girl. Jayne wasn't her keeper.

"Who do you think's on the phone with Ellie?" Grams's head was turned, and Jayne knew she was straining to hear her little sister's conversation. Grams always told her she tried to live vicariously through her beautiful granddaughters.

"Don't know, don't care."

Ellie could live her life. Jayne was too busy trying to tread water in her own life.

She felt a cool hand circle her ankle. It was a surprisingly strong hand for a woman in her seventh decade on Earth. "You know you can talk to me about anything, right, Jayne?" Grams peered at her over her pink frames. "Anything. Boys, Ellie, your life right now. I'm an ear and a shoulder when you need one."

"Thanks, Grams." It had been two months of not talking about the accident. She wasn't about to start now. "Yeah, I know."

"Good. Just had to put that out there in case you didn't know." She patted Jayne's toes before pushing away from her. For the next minute, Grams battled another coughing fit. Then she took another sip of her drink and another drag from her cigarette. "I know your dad is there for you. He's my son. I raised him right. But with that mother of yours . . ."

She shook her head and whistled, long and low.

Grams's feelings for Jayne's mom weren't exactly news. But Gen *was* her mom. She was what she was. Jayne concentrated on scooping a ladybug out of the pool with a nearby leaf.

"You going to summer school?" Grams rasped.

Jayne grimaced. Her head was down, so Grams didn't see it. She darted a look up. Nope, Grams hadn't seen it. "Yep, I start school tomorrow."

"Good, good. I know how much you like school."

Jayne stayed silent. She used to like school.

That was, until she got the four C's and two B's.

Jayne started feeling a burning sensation in the pit of her stomach. She knew what it was. She'd been feeling it ever since she'd gotten her report card.

She hadn't told anyone about her grades. Not Tom. Not her folks. Not Ellie.

Jayne concentrated on the ladybug as it opened and closed its wings, drying. She couldn't keep this grade thing to herself. That 2.3 was eating her up. Where'd that put her? Number fifty out of seven hundred in the class? What kind of standing was that?

What kind of future was that?

She couldn't tell anyone. If she told her mom, she'd get a lecture about goal-setting and making it in today's economy.

If she told her dad, he'd tell her mom.

If she told Ellie . . . she couldn't tell Ellie. Ellie would start asking her stupid questions again, like, "Do you think you'll still get into Harvard, Jaynie?"

How the frick would she know?

But her grams? Jayne could tell her. She wouldn't say anything.

Heck, she'd probably forget by the time *Wheel of Fortune* came on tonight.

"So. Grams." Jayne cleared her throat and focused on the ladybug opening and closing its wings. "I kind of got a bad report card."

She took a deep breath and, for the first time since she'd flushed the Palm Desert High letter down the toilet, said the unspeakable aloud.

"Two B's." She swallowed and took a deep breath to force the rest of the words out. "And four C's."

There. She'd finally said it. She might as well say the rest, too.

"There's no way I'm going to be valedictorian now." Another swallow, another breath. "Who knows if I'm even in the top ten percent of the class? Or even up for that Senior Student award anymore?"

Was she talking too loud? She looked over at Ellie, whose yellow bikini top pushed her boobs up all perfectly. In a quieter voice, she added, "Harvard's definitely not going to give me the time of day now."

The last words were really a question. She waited for Grams to say she was an idiot. That Harvard was still in the cards.

She waited. And waited. The ladybug flew off.

A raspy snore finally broke the wait. Jayne looked up to see the Bloody Mary tipped over into the pool, the red liquid mixing with the chlorinated water.

16

C'MON, TOMMY." Jayne fell back onto her bed, the cordless under her chin. She turned on the TV and flipped through the channels, the volume on mute. Tom hated it when she talked to him with the TV on. "I have to be there for three hours a day, five days a week."

Summer school started tomorrow. And Jayne was dreading it.

Possibly worse than the time she had to go to the dentist to get all four wisdom teeth pulled freshman year.

"And how is me being there three hours a day, five days a week, going to help you?" Tom asked.

"By keeping me company at the break."

"That's only fifteen minutes."

"We can pass notes."

"Jayne, you don't pass notes. It goes against your 'shh, the teacher's talking' code."

"A girl can change." She had one more way to get him to say yes. She just had to be careful about how she phrased it. "Taking classes now can help you stock up on more honors classes in the fall, you know."

"What's the point? You're set as valedictorian, right?" There seemed to be an open-ended question there. Did he know about her grades? She felt her eyelid twitch.

And Tom finding out about her grades was somehow fifty times worse than if her parents did.

Why, she didn't know. She just . . . felt that it would be. Worse.

Embarrassing, somehow. Like he'd be disappointed in her.

"Jayne, are you watching TV?"

"Why?"

"You didn't answer my question. About you being valedictorian."

Guiltily, Jayne clicked off the TV. She flipped on her stomach and stared at the shadows the tree outside was making against her wall.

"You never know, right? I could mess up calculus next year." *Cover your tracks, Jayne, cover your tracks.*

"Right. You never mess up anything." Was that pride in his voice?

"Okay then, maybe my scientific calculator starts going wonky on me and gives me all the wrong answers?" She tried to laugh off the answer. It was hard, though. There was nothing to laugh about when it came to those fourth-quarter grades. Or the doors that were now shut because of them. "Or maybe I'll decide to cut down on my honors classes, take that photography class I'm always thinking about."

In a softer voice, she added, "Maybe I won't even take any honors."

This was the first time she actually voiced that thought aloud.

She'd been thinking about it for a while. Ever since she started to think hard about why, exactly, she couldn't be an average teenage girl.

Like a certain younger sister in this house.

"Yeah, right." He laughed. For like three minutes straight.

Giving up on honors classes wasn't *that* stupid an idea.

Was it?

"If you take summer school with me, I promise I'll bring . . ." She searched her memory for his favorite foods. There were a lot to choose from. "Those turkey jerky strips you like."

"Nah. Too salty."

"Cheetos?"

"Too messy."

She was almost out of food groups. "Twinkies."

"Now you're talking."

"Good. I'll bring a box of Twinkies tomorrow."

"A box of Twinkies a week." Before she could disagree, he added, "And those kung fu movies I like and you don't? You've gotta watch five of them with me this summer."

She would watch five hundred if that meant he'd come.

Not only would she be in a boring class for three hours a day for five weeks, but she would also be back on campus for the first time since school ended.

Since the last day of school. When someone put pictures of car crash victims on her locker.

And wrote KILLER in red paint.

"Deal."

"Hey!" Tom sounded like he hadn't expected her to cave in to the kung fu movies. "Not so fast. I'm still negotiating here. I also want to get out of all chick flicks for the rest of my life, a lifetime of you never doing your happy dance when you get a higher grade than me . . ."

Tom listed his demands. Jayne stuck by her guns.

He got Twinkies and five kung fu movies.

She got a friend in hostile territory.

"Okay, people, we'll take a short break. Get some caffeine, get some sugar. Maybe find some spare brain cells. Meet you back here in"—Mr. Munroe looked over his shoulder, his comb-over more apparent from the back—"twenty minutes."

Twenty minutes. Not nearly enough time to recuperate from the last hour and a half. Hopis, Navajos, Papagos, Pimas. There were a lot of Native American tribes to remember. And each was more boring than the last.

And Mr. Munroe talking about them—actually, reading about them straight from the book, word for word—was killing her brain. Which was a feat, since her brain had felt numb for months.

Today it felt like he was lobotomizing her, one word at a time.

"You feel like going to a movie tonight?"

Tom stretched, his long frame taking over about three rows.

"Can't. I've got my thing after this." There were still a couple of kids in the class, lingering over horror books or text messaging. No one needed to know what the state was making her do at Outreach Arizona.

Jayne got up, checking her money situation. Time to reboot her brain. She started walking into the hall.

"You're not trying to get out of your promise, right? About the five kung fu movies?"

"No, I'm not getting out . . ."

She stopped talking. Words were failing her.

Lori was by the soda machine, kicking the dispenser, saying in an overly loud voice, "I pushed the diet, it should give me diet. Not root beer, and definitely not regular root beer."

Jenna sat at the table in the vending area, a closed bag of Fritos in front of her. She wasn't wearing any makeup, and she had on a wrinkled T-shirt. Her usually bouncy, shiny curls were dull and frizzy, gathered haphazardly on top of her head.

They hadn't seen Jayne yet. She turned and headed in the opposite direction.

"Jayne, I can get you your food." Tom was right next to her, his arm pressing into hers. "What do you want?"

"That's okay. I'm good." She hugged her wallet to her chest, her steps fast and furious.

"No you're not," he scoffed.

No, she wasn't.

All she knew was that the vending machines were in enemy territory.

And she was the enemy.

17

I Have Bologna on white bread, a Hostess cupcake, a pack of Twizzlers, and a bag of Doritos. What do you have to trade?"

"Chicken on whole wheat, an apple, a protein shake, and pita chips."

"Yuck." Meadow started opening her sandwich. "What's up with the healthfest?"

"I started basketball camp and feel really slow on the court." Darian patted his flat stomach. "Time to trim down."

Jayne cradled the can of Diet Pepsi in her hands, her head down as she stared blankly at one of her mom's tabloids she'd brought with her. She never ate lunch since she didn't usually have an appetite. Instead, she nursed twelve ounces of pop and stared at the same magazine page.

Celebrity love lives and catfights. Nowadays, they were the only stories she really read. She hadn't even begun to read her Arizona history book.

And the class had started four days ago. And they had a test next week.

"Hey, princess."

Jayne turned the page, slurping the last of her pop.

"Jayne."

She looked up. Darian was smiling at her. He pushed his Ziploc of pita chips toward her. "Want any?"

She shook her head. She gave him a small smile. "No thanks. I'm covered."

"Yeah, Darian, eating those will totally ruin her cred as an Ana."

"Ana?" Jayne asked the question before she realized that doing so would suck her into conversation with Meadow.

"Yeah." Meadow squeezed her cupcake before licking the cream with her tongue. "You're anorexic, aren't you?"

Jayne was too surprised to answer right away. She looked down at her hands holding the pop. They were bonier than usual, her wrists standing out in sharp relief against her skin. She'd had to wear a sweatshirt over her jeans today because the waistband was too big and gapped away from her skin.

But they still stayed up, so she hadn't thought she'd lost that much weight.

Then again, her mom had told her she looked good this morning. "To be your age again, Jayne. A size zero and the whole world in front of me."

She was far from a size zero. But her athletic size-eight body had definitely shrunk. And sitting here getting called anorexic and having her mom compliment her on seeing the bones . . .

She didn't have enough money for anything other than the pop. She scanned the food in front of the other two. "Feel like sharing that second cupcake?"

Meadow pushed the cake toward her.

A chair scratched against the linoleum floor. "So, Princess Jayne, what made you lose your appetite?"

She smiled at Darian. Somehow, "Princess Jayne" sounded cute. Not vindictive, like Tattoo Girl's "princess." She didn't feel like going into the accident, so she settled on a distant second. "I've got some mom issues."

"Amen, sister." Meadow slid her bag of Doritos across the table, the opening facing Jayne. "I can totally relate to the mom thing." In an exaggerated whisper, she said, "Mom's the one who called the cops on me about the Ritalin, the witch."

"Jayne, what's your mom like? I don't see *you* being a Ritalin dealer." Darian grinned at Jayne around a bite of sandwich.

"She's just a mom, I guess, with usual mom flaws." Times a billion. But she didn't want to get into that with these two. She didn't feel like getting into how her mom was Gen Thompkins, local celebrity.

"Like what? Name one." Meadow sucked at a cheesy thumb. "Amuse us."

Name one? That was tough.

A thousand were darting through Jayne's head.

"Like she only wants me taking honors classes. Nothing else. I wanted to take a photography class freshman year, and she didn't understand how that would get me into H ... college."

"So why didn't you take the photography class?" Meadow looked like she didn't understand a word Jayne had just said.

"Because my mom didn't want me to."

"So?" Meadow slurped the rest of her root beer. "Your mom isn't registering for classes, right?"

"No, but . . ."

"And you go to public school, right, so she doesn't have to pay for your books?"

"We have a really good public school where I live. Best in Arizona."

"And the books are free?"

Jayne nodded.

"So what's the problem?"

Jayne thought about it. Actually, there was no problem. Gen wasn't living Jayne's life. Making her day-to-day decisions. She could sign up for whatever and take however many honors she wanted to. And the electives she wanted to take.

Like photography.

But knowing her mom, she'd do something to control the situation.

"If I don't sign up for what she wants, she might take away my bus pass." As soon as Jayne said it, she knew it sounded lame.

"No car?" Meadow raised an eyebrow. "Your boyfriend drive you places?"

Jayne's cheeks got hot. "I don't have a boyfriend." She had nothing to be ashamed of. "No need for one. I live on the bus route."

"Ah-so," Darian said, and Jayne immediately thought of Tom and his kung fu movies. "You use boys for their cars, eh?"

Jayne laughed. "Whatever. The bus and I get along just fine."

"But the *bus*?" Meadow said the word like Jayne had just said "rat-infested sewer."

"You're not the only princess around here, Jayne," Darian

said. "Our little Meadow here has a family that's richer than Trump himself."

"Whatever." Meadow put her hand a few inches from her face as she checked out her nails. "The Olsen twins, maybe."

Jayne flipped off the TV and wondered if it was possible for brain cells to die from watching too much TV. She'd just finished a three-hour marathon of *Gilligan's Island* and now she was staring up at the ceiling.

Not doing homework.

Not checking e-mail.

Not going to the movies with Ellie. Who had gone without her. Who hadn't even bothered to ask her along.

The only thing to think about were the fifty weeks that were left until she was done with Outreach Arizona. The second most boring place on earth, after Arizona history class.

Darian was okay, she guessed. Meadow was . . . tolerable. Ryan ignorable.

But she didn't need the constant reminder about the accident.

That left her mother's Xanax. She'd been taking it on and off for a couple of weeks, making sure she didn't take too many so her mom wouldn't notice the pilfering.

Her folks were downstairs playing *Scene It* with some friends. Her dad had come up three times already to ask her if she wanted to play. All three times, she'd shaken her head and turned up the TV as her answer.

Jayne picked up *Animal Farm* from her nightstand. She'd started reading it back in April, before . . . Before. She was ten pages into it.

She'd read only a page in the last two months. Tonight wasn't much better. She read two sentences before she put it away and decided to just stare at the ceiling.

It wasn't like it mattered if she finished it or not. It was a book on the Harvard reading list. A list she'd downloaded two years ago. She'd read 132 of the books on it so far.

Out of 300.

But those 132 books weren't going to get her into Harvard. Her grades would've.

Would've. Could've. Should've.

Jayne felt the bed vibrate. Britney ambled up from her napping spot at the foot of the bed and climbed up Jayne's leg before curling up on her chest. Sometimes Jayne had a feeling Britney thought she was a cat.

But she didn't try to move the pug. Her twenty-pound body wasn't comfortable, but it was comforting.

Jayne scratched behind an ear. "Hello, little buddy."

The pug looked at her with her head cocked to one side, like she was trying to decipher what Jayne had said. She put her head on her paws, her bright eyes staring at her human servant.

Instead of feeling loved, Jayne felt lonely. Tom was busy with basketball camp this week, so she only got to see him in summer school.

Britney started snoring, doggy breath exhaling on Jayne's mouth. Jayne eased out from under the pup. She looked at the TV. Nah. She was getting bedsores from watching that thing. She looked at her computer. Maybe Tom had e-mailed her?

She clicked on the computer. No e-mails from Tom. Then again, he'd said he'd be busy with that camp.

She did have one message. From an E. Thompkins.

When'd Ellie get a new e-mail? Her sister was CalvinSucks@yahoo.com. She pretty much used it for sending Jayne chain letters. She hadn't in a while, though, ever since Jayne had starting living the life of a hermit.

Jayne clicked on the e-mail. There was only a hyperlink on the page: www.cutepuppypics.com.

For once, Ellie had sent her something Jayne might actually look at.

She clicked on the link.

And forgot how to breathe.

A picture of Jayne was centered on the page. It looked like it was the photo from the junior class yearbook.

In red, bleeding letters, were the words "Most Likely to Go to Hell."

18

JAYNE FELT LIKE she'd been drugged.

It took her a couple of tries, but she finally slipped her key into the lock, turned it, and used her weight to open one of the double doors that led into the Thompkins home.

Friggin' fug. She was *tired*.

Then again, it'd been a long day. Three hours at summer school, listening to Mr. Munroe drone on about the four C's of Arizona: copper, cotton, something, and something. She'd tuned out by the third C and doodled for most of the class.

Then she'd spent the next six hours answering Maria's phone at Outreach Arizona. (Jayne wanted out of that place. Six hours a day, five days a week, would get her out in ten months instead of twelve. She'd done the math. In between doodling on her paper-bag-covered history book.)

The day had been really busy because Maria'd gotten a lot of calls. Some event was happening this weekend and everyone wanted to cover their butts with Maria.

Not that Jayne blamed them. Maria was a tough cookie. She didn't take "no"—or "I screwed up"—for an answer.

Crazy how going from watching TV all day to staying out for nine hours wiped a girl out.

Jayne slipped out of her Nikes and headed to the kitchen. She was starving. And her Diet Pepsis and Meadow's cupcakes weren't cutting it so much.

Ellie stood at the island, a wooden spoon in one hand, a glass mixing bowl in front of her. Her hair was tied out of her face with a ponytail holder that looked like a tiara.

Figured.

"Where've you been?"

"Out." Jayne grabbed a yogurt and a bag of pretzels.

It looked like Ellie was making the Thompkinses' Secret Chocolate Chip Cookie recipe. It was made with sugar substitutes—even the chocolate chips—so Ellie wouldn't go into diabetic shock.

Twice a year, Ellie and Jayne would make it and get sick from the cookie dough.

"I'm almost done." Ellie didn't look up. Her voice was strained, and Jayne was quite aware she was the cause of it. She didn't give a crap, though. Too tired. "Wanna scoop?"

Jayne knew this was an olive branch, but she didn't want to take it. She wasn't ready to take it. She was too tired to take it.

"I think I just want to go to bed." She walked out of the kitchen. She didn't know what devil made her say over her shoulder: "You're the only one around here who has time to scoop cookies."

Behind her, there was silence. Then, "At least I have a life, you frickin' zombie!"

But Jayne kept going. She didn't have the energy to say

what she was thinking: *Not without that FIT scholarship, you don't.*

This zombie had to go to bed. Ellie could fend for herself.

One container of yogurt and a quarter bag of pretzels later, Jayne stared at her computer monitor.

Tom was online. There he was, BasketTrack12. He thought he'd been so cool when he'd come up with a name that combined his two sports and his jersey number.

Jayne stared at his message.

BasketTrack12: Hey. You there?

She clicked onto the instant messenger and made sure that Tom couldn't see she was on. She inhaled a shuddery breath.

She was officially hiding from Tom. Her best friend.

Right now, she was too tired to be a friend. Much less someone's best one.

Before she clicked out of the messaging program, someone else popped up:

IHeartBB: this is darian. can i please speak to jayne?

Her heartbeat felt like it did when she'd just had a really long volley on the tennis court. She poised her fingertips over her keyboard. What to say, what to say . . .

Britney4Ever: Dork. Hey. I'm here.

She read over what she'd written. Erased "Dork" before she sent it. She didn't know him *that* well. Not Tom well.

IHeartBB: feel up to a movie?

A movie? Like a date movie? Her heart sped up. Like the way it did when she drank a Red Bull before a tennis match.

Play it cool, Jayne. Play it cool.

Britney4Ever: Depends. Which one?

IHeartBB: the one with the beekeeper bilionare. i hear its real funny. tonight sound good?

Jayne ignored the spelling and grammar errors. Darian didn't seem like the type who cared too much about that stuff.

Britney4Ever: Too tired right now. Tomorrow maybe?

Jayne hesitated for about five heartbeats before she finally sent the message. Was she saying yes to a date? The girl who'd never had time for a date because she had a test to study for/a paper to write/Harvard to prepare for?

She waited for a reply. Five minutes later, still nothing.

She went to the bathroom. Brushed her teeth.

Ten minutes later, her gums were sore and she knew she couldn't put off looking for Darian's response any longer.

IHeartBB: sorry. took out trash. mom pissed. yeah, saturday works. what time?

Jayne was about to put down a time when she remembered. Tomorrow was her parents' Fourth of July party. Food, friends, and stilted fun.

Crap.

Britney4Ever: I forgot. I have a family thing tomorrow. A Fourth of July thing. You can come if you want.

A second after she sent it, she wished she could take it back and edit her words. With lightning speed, she typed out:

Britney4Ever: Or not. Come here, I mean. I can do the movie next weekend. My treat.

She hit SEND. Darian was going to think she was blowing him off. Knowing her luck, he'd give up trying to ask her out. Like that Norwegian foreign exchange student, Petter. Tall, dark, handsome, with dimples in all the right spots. She'd been a freshman, he'd been a junior. He'd asked her to go to a hockey game; she had said yes.

Then she'd realized she'd double-booked him with a debate and she'd asked for a rain check.

He'd never asked her out again.

A ding sounded.

IHeartBB: girls dont treat guys. and im good with families. what time should I bring my world famous three bean dip?

19

CANNONBALL!!"

Jayne watched Tom fling himself for what must've been the twentieth time from the top of the Thompkinses' man-made waterfall. If he wasn't careful, he was going to give himself diarrhea. Again.

Like he'd done at Jayne's fifth-grade birthday party.

Jayne walked over to one of the long rented tables crammed with fried chicken, potato salad, and every kind of potato chip known to humankind. She snagged a Diet Pepsi from an ice-filled tin tied with red-white-and-blue crepe paper. The tablecloth, a vinyl version of the American flag, was already splattered with salsa.

It was eight o'clock, and the sunlight was almost gone. The Thompkinses' annual Fourth of July bash was officially in full swing.

The only thing that was making this a less-than-perfect night was the person who was still missing. Darian.

"Cannonball!"

Jayne rolled her eyes and walked toward the house.

Tom was going to be one sorry dude if he didn't cut off the cannonballs soon.

Inside, the kitchen clock said 8:05. She checked the answering machine. Nope, no blinking message light.

She ran up the stairs and turned on her computer. Nope, no e-mail message.

Breathe, Jayne. Relax. It's not like Darian's helping you finish a class project that's due in an hour.

She sat in the dark room, hearing the strains of some girl rock song and random laughter from one of the dozens of guests outside. The average person would've been stoked to go back to the party. Or put on a bathing suit to go swimming.

Jayne stayed put. For one, Miss Challen, her guidance counselor, was out there.

Yeah, *that* Challen, propped up on a chaise longue. She'd been there all night, cradling the same margarita and laughing a little too hard and long with some guy.

Proof that being older and single wasn't a pretty thing.

She hadn't tried to talk to Jayne at all. Then again, Jayne kept making sure to keep the length of the pool between them.

She started to turn on the TV when the doorbell rang. Jayne walked to the window and peered down, but the porch roof kept her from seeing who it was.

Butterflies began fluttering in her stomach. Jayne tried to walk as slowly as she could back downstairs. She ended up skipping to the door.

Opening it, she saw Diane, her mom's assistant.

"Hey, Di—"

She didn't get the rest of the words out. The person behind Diane, a smug smile on her face, made talking really difficult.

It was Lori. Lori Parnell.

The Wicked Witch of the West.

"What do you mean she's Diane's stepdaughter?"

"Young lady, keep your voice down."

Jayne had cornered her mom by the stone grill outside. They were behind a bougainvillea bush that hid them.

And their argument.

"Fine." In a lower voice that was just as pissed, Jayne overly enunciated her next question: "What is she do-ing here?"

"Don't take that tone, little girl." Her mother crossed her arms, her silicone boobs showing even more cleavage in the black bikini. "I didn't know that Lori was Diane's stepdaughter. God, Diane just got remarried a couple of weeks ago. I didn't know the name of the guy or his history."

Which made sense, actually. Gen wasn't big into details. Especially if they had nothing to do with her.

"Hey, stranger."

Jayne turned to see Darian walking up behind her, his Hawaiian swim trunks showing off muscular calves and his open button-down showing off a six-pack.

He almost made her forget who was here.

Almost.

"Hello there." Gen's voice was no-nonsense. "I'm Gen Thompkins, Jayne's mom. You're . . . ?"

"Darian, Mrs. Thompkins."

"And you know Jayne from . . ." Gen, the consummate interviewer, led with another open-ended question.

"The Outreach program, ma'am. Building up my college résumé, just like Jayne here."

"That's good to hear." Gen's tone was distracted. She lifted her hand to wave at someone. "If you'll excuse me, Damon, my producer just got here and I need to speak to him about a few story ideas. Excuse me, will you?"

She didn't wait for an answer.

"Your mom is Gen Thompkins?"

Jayne raised her eyebrows. "What does it matter?"

They stood staring at each other in silence for a few moments, Jayne unsure how to take Darian knowing who her mom was.

"Feel like taking a dip?" He tilted his head toward the pool, a smile emerging on his lips.

Jayne turned, taking in the scene. From the "Marco" and "Polo!" she heard, she could guess what was going on. In the dark, it was hard to make out who was out there.

She could, however, make out Ellie in the Jacuzzi, holding court with a group of her mall buddies.

Ellie's eyes were fixed on them.

"I don't have my swimsuit on."

"No worries." Before she knew it, strong arms slid under her knees and behind her shoulder blades.

"Aaahh!" Jayne clasped her arms around his neck, afraid that her head was about to connect with the concrete. "Darian! Put me down!"

"What's that you say?" Jayne opened her eyes to find herself a few inches from his face. He was smiling, two dimples creasing the sides of his cheeks. "You want me to put you down?"

She felt a smile pulling at her lips. She nodded. "Yes, please."

He shrugged, and her body went up and down with the effort. Gorgeous *and* strong. "Alrighty, then."

Before she knew what he was doing, he stepped up to the edge of the pool and jumped in—with her still in his arms. About a second before he did it, Jayne realized what he was about to do and took a breath. Which was the only reason she didn't drown when the water came up over her head.

When her head broke the surface, she heard Darian laughing before she saw him.

"You're such a jerk!" Her laughter took the edge off the words.

"Yeah?" He splashed her. She splashed him back in reflex.

"Yeah."

"I got you in here, didn't I?" He gave her a slow smile. "And I got you to smile, right?"

From the corner of her eye, she saw Tom treading water a few yards away, his mouth in a tight line.

"Hey," she said, turning to Tom. But then she stopped. Lori had her arms reaching out to grab Tom around the shoulders.

"Gotcha!"

A white-hot poker seemed to jam through Jayne's heart and stomach. Before she could catch a breath, someone called her name.

Loudly.

Angrily.

Jayne looked around to see bright orange toenails in turquoise slides. Tilting her head back, she saw her mother's angry face.

In a stage whisper, her mother spat out, "Get out of that pool right this minute, young lady."

Even with all her senses still reeling from Darian, Tom, and Lori, she knew her mom wasn't mad about her being in the pool with her clothes on.

The day of reckoning had come.

20

Jayne barely had time to wrap a beach towel around her torso before Gen Thompkins took her elbow. She hissed low enough so only Jayne could hear her words. "C's? You got C's? Not that the B's were any better, but C's? What were you thinking?"

Jayne had known this day was coming. She just wished it wasn't today, in front of Darian and Lori and a crowd. She kept her head down. Not wanting to see pity or, in Lori's case, glee.

Her mom led her through the backyard and through the double doors off the patio. Into her dad's study.

Out of everyone's earshot.

Once the door closed behind them, Jayne said calmly, "I just couldn't think straight last quarter, you know?"

"No, I don't know. What I *do* know is—"

Her dad came in through the French doors, an open oxford shirt over his swimsuit.

"What I *do* know," her mom continued, ignoring him, "is you're going to work so hard to make this up you're going to be wondering what a good night's sleep feels like."

"What's this about, Gen?" Her dad came over to stand next to Jayne. "Angie Challen said I should come in here."

Angie Challen. What a twit. Jayne closed her eyes briefly, trying to forget about all the emotions already coursing through her.

She had a battle to prepare for.

"Your daughter here earned a 2.3 GPA last quarter." Gen crossed her arms, her head shaking from side to side as if she couldn't believe what she'd just said.

"I was wondering why we'd gotten Ellie's report card and not yours." He put an arm around Jayne's shoulders. "How're you holding up, kid?"

"Oh, suck it up, Sean." Gen crossed her arms, her gold bangles clanking together. "Jayne needs some tough love, not your touchy-feely crap."

Sean looked straight at his wife, keeping his arm around Jayne's shoulders. "Grades aren't love, Gen."

"I know grades aren't love, but caring about her future is." She pointed at Jayne. "How's she going to get into a good school with a 2.3?"

"That was only one quarter. Jaynie already had over a 4.0. Angie says she still has over a 4.0. So what if it's not a 4.25?"

"So what?" Gen sneered. "If she wanted to go to a state school"—she said the words like they were dirty and distaste-ful—"a 4.0 would get her in, no problem."

Sean squeezed Jayne tighter. "What's so wrong with a state school, Gen?"

Gen gestured around with her outspread hands. "Look around. We could've been living in New York, me at a cable station, you at Columbia, if we'd gotten an Ivy League education."

"I think we have a pretty damn good life." He squeezed Jayne closer to him. "And we're not hundreds of thousands of dollars in debt, either."

Jayne's mom looked like she was about to launch herself at her husband of seventeen years and claw his eyes out. Jayne let herself sink deeper into her dad's side.

Gen took a deep breath and leaned forward, her hands on her hips. She seemed to be scrutinizing her toenail polish. "We have guests right now, so we'll be picking this conversation up later, young lady. Figure out how to get those grades up." She looked at Jayne. "Maybe you can retake the quarter."

Jayne didn't say anything.

After she'd gotten her report card, she'd looked up the student handbook online. Only D's or worse could be retaken.

Her mom avoided eye contact as she breezed through the French doors, the fringe of her sarong whipping angrily behind her.

If hate and loathing had a smell, Gen Thompkins would've been equal parts rotten egg and skunk.

"How're you holding up, Jaynie?"

She pulled away from her dad and pushed the heels of her hands into her eyes. She shrugged. Did it matter how she was doing?

Her dad pulled her hands away from her face and kissed her forehead. "Now don't go gouging your eyes out. Your mom will cool down and get her senses back. Why don't you get back out to the party?"

He turned her around to face the doors. "Looks like your friend out there's lonely."

"Tom?" She took a deep breath and adjusted the straps of her tank top. Tom would know how to calm her down.

He'd seen enough of Gen's tantrums to become an expert at picking up the pieces.

"No, that other young man. The one who likes picking you up."

Oh yeah. *That* young man.

Instead of going back to the pool, Jayne went out the door that led to the downstairs bathroom. She had to check to see if her face showed anything.

Like the fact that she'd just been chewed out by a woman who skinned puppy dogs to make fur coats.

As Jayne stepped into the hallway, she collided into a wide, tan chest.

"You okay?"

She looked up to see the brown eyes that were beginning to get imprinted on her mind.

"Yeah. Just some family drama." She tried to crack a smile, but it was still too soon after the fight. "Sorry about that."

"Hey, I understand." She felt Darian's hand go underneath her chin. Gentle pressure forced her to meet his eyes again. "But you're okay?"

She felt her pulse thrumming in her throat. He really was too good-looking. And nice.

Too good to be true, a tiny voice singsonged in the back of her head.

"I'm okay. Thank you."

"So formal." He moved his head closer to hers, until his

breath was brushing her lips. "Let's see what we can do to fix that."

In the next instant, his lips covered hers and a hand moved to the small of her back. She gave in to the warmth of his mouth, tentatively.

Then she felt it.

His tongue touching her lips.

Did he want her to open her mouth? Her head was swimming with the fact that she was kissing a hottie. Here. In her house.

This was only the third male mouth on hers in her entire life. And one didn't even count (well, it could, but that would be utterly disgusting considering it was her dad's when he used to kiss her good night when she was little).

The only problem she had in her life right now was whether or not she was supposed to let Darian's tongue in her mouth. That, and her brain didn't seem to want to shut off long enough for her to just enjoy the damn kiss!

"Well, lookie here."

Jayne pulled away so fast from Darian that her elbow bumped a picture on the wall, unhooking it from its nail. Reflexively, she turned around and caught it between the wall and her body.

Tom stood in the hallway, wearing that pissy look she'd seen at the pool.

Beside him was Lori.

Lori, who should've been wearing green greasepaint to warn people about her toxic personality.

The one who'd been sending her those e-mails. And those text messages.

"Excuse me." Those two words dripped with saccharin. Lori

pushed her way between Jayne and Darian. "I need to use the little girls' room."

As Lori headed down the hallway, she threw back, "I'm surprised at you, Jayne."

Lori was looking for a fight. Usually, Jayne wouldn't have given her one. She wasn't that kind of girl.

But tonight, she'd been blindsided by an enemy, thrown into the pool, given pissy looks by her best friend, yelled at by her mother, kissed by a hottie, and now ordered around by this witch.

She'd had enough. "That I actually enjoy the male persuasion, unlike you?"

For a brief moment, Lori looked surprised. Before Jayne could feel good about getting the upper hand, though, the witch regained her composure. "Oh, I enjoy the males. I enjoy them a lot."

Lori's smile was creepy. Like Jack Nicholson's in that *Shining* movie. Right before he went on a killing spree.

"I'm just surprised that you're able to kiss anyone at all after killing Jenna's sister and all."

If Lori was eaten by a pack of coyotes, would anyone even miss her? If Lori was lost in the Andes with five other people and someone had to be killed for the others to eat, how would they murder Lori?

After Lori's parting words, Jayne had gone up to her room. Attempted to calm down. Attempted to stop wanting to rip Lori's face off.

"Hey." Darian's voice came from behind her. She turned, her eyes not meeting his.

"Jayne, I knew already."

"You knew what?"

"I knew about the girl. And the accident."

She finally looked at him. His eyes were warm and sympathetic. Like Tom's had been. The only difference was that she didn't want to punch Darian in the face for cavorting with an enemy.

"You knew?"

"Yeah." He pushed away from the doorway and ran a hand through his hair. It was a little less spiky today. The chlorine had a way of doing that. "Maria told me."

A flash of . . . anger? shock? . . . popped through Jayne. "I thought that was confidential."

"I was in her office one day and she sort of let it slip about what had happened. She didn't mean to tell me anything." He put a hand over his heart. "Honest. Don't be mad at her."

For the second time that day, she felt betrayed. First Tom, now Maria.

But this betrayal didn't cut quite as deep as Tom's had.

Small consolation, though.

"What I'm trying to say, though, is that what that girl said out there didn't mean anything." He was close. Close enough to put his hand on Jayne's cheek. "And that I like you a lot."

She thought maybe her heart was going to drop into her stomach. That hand felt good. It felt like it was grounding her in this topsy-turvy world of disappointed mothers, useless dads, turncoat best friends, and loose-lipped counselors.

And for the second time that day, Jayne Lee Thompkins kissed a boy.

This time, she opened her mouth.

21

THE MUZAK IN THIS PLACE was driving Jayne nuts. She picked up another *National Geographic*, flipping through it but not really looking at it. Instead, she looked at her watch for the hundredth time.

Larry the Fairy was running late.

She stopped on a page that showed the flattest, starkest cliff she'd seen in her life. The caption read "Inishmore Island, Aran Islands, Ireland."

That lonely, stark place looked like it would've been a one hundred percent improvement over this land of seventies furniture, gray carpet, and tropical rain forest.

This office sort of reminded her of Val's office. Except the plants here were real and very shiny.

A door opened around the corner. "Jayne? You ready?"

Larry came out, his hair going in every which direction, his big bug eyes popping out of his head. He was wearing a Hawaiian shirt, khakis, and flip-flops.

Larry sure didn't know how to dress for his clients. Or in general.

"Yeah." She put the magazine under her arm and walked past him. After the weekend she'd had, she didn't give a crud about putting up appearances. She wore a pair of sweats with a hole at the knee and a black Metallica shirt that had been her dad's back in college.

Her mom had tried to make her change her clothes, but she'd failed. Anyway, Gen had already gotten her way once today. And that was Jayne's quota.

She was here to see Larry the Fairy, wasn't she? To help straighten her out, as her mom put it. "Jayne, I don't know what's gotten into you, but you need to get back on track. School starts in a month and I need to see A's from you."

Her mom didn't insist on driving her here, though. It was like she'd made a pact with her dad to keep some distance from her. Jayne could tell her mom wanted to say stuff to her, though. She had that pinched look she got when something was bothering her.

Larry clicked a pen, a noise that made Jayne stop with her Gen thoughts. The hum of the humidifier was the only other noise in the room.

"How was your week?"

"Fine."

He nodded and just sat there. The faithful humidifier hummed its song over in the corner, and Jayne let her mind wander.

Okay, Jayne. You better think of something before you tell him something out of sheer boredom.

That's when she came up with Shakespeare soliloquies she'd had to memorize back in Freshman Lit.

What'll it be today? Um ... Polonius, maybe.

Brevity is the soul of wit ... Wait, no, there was something else before that. What was it?

"It looks like you're in the middle of some deep thoughts there, Jayne." Larry was watering one of his many plants.

"Yeah." She looked at her fingernails, bitten down to the quick. "I was just thinking about what color I was going to paint my nails. I've got it narrowed down to Berrylicious and Berry Frost."

Larry made a sound in the back of his throat as he drizzled water over the plant. "Sounds like you have plans tonight."

"Nope." The word came out before she realized she'd said it. At his raised eyebrow, she shrugged. "There aren't too many plans in Jayne Thompkins's life nowadays. No big deal."

Even she heard the forced flippancy in those last few words. She tore her gaze off of Larry and opened up the magazine she'd brought in.

Feeling like she'd said too much already, Jayne didn't talk for the rest of the hour.

22

"WHY DO YOU need me here again?"

This chair was really digging into her in all the wrong places. It had been almost a half hour since Jayne had come to her mom's studio, and she was bored.

And a little pissed.

Her mom still hadn't told her what she was doing here. And the mystery was sort of eating at Jayne.

Whatever the reason was, it couldn't be good.

Gen was across from her at her immaculate desk, scribbling on a yellow legal pad and concentrating on whatever was written on the Post-it she was transcribing.

It was midweek. Her mom had given her the lame excuse that she needed someone to file her clippings. Diane was out of town, doing some legwork on a story for Gen.

Filing had taken ten minutes. Somehow, Jayne didn't think she was here because the world would end if clippings weren't filed.

Jayne had a feeling that she was here to repent for her grades. And for yelling at her mom.

"I just thought it would be good to get you out of the house. Give you a change of scenery." Gen pulled her knee up and leaned against it as she continued to write. She had two hours until she went on air and was wearing a velour tracksuit. A salmon suit was on the hook behind her door, freshly pressed.

Jayne thought it was her mom's best outfit. It made her look professional. Approachable. Even kind.

It was a miracle worker, in other words.

"I have to be at the Outreach program in, like, forty-five minutes." Not that Jayne was aching to answer phones and be bored. But another day meant she was closer to being done with it.

Plus, Darian would be there.

"This won't take long." Her mom scribbled her last note before dialing a few numbers.

"Cameron? Yeah, Jayne's here. Can we swing by? Great."

Jayne was confused. She stayed seated as her mom got up and smoothed the creases from her pants. She looked at Jayne expectantly. "Coming?"

"Why are we going to see Cameron?" Cameron Tolliver was the producer of her mom's Saturday show. She'd said hi to him a couple of times, but they'd never had a conversation that lasted longer than three words.

"You'll see." And with that mysterious response, she pulled Jayne up and guided her to the door.

Cameron's office was smaller than her mom's with a big poster of some naked chick in the middle of a stack of tires. Classy. Then again, she hadn't expected anything less from a guy who'd stripped off his swim trunks at midnight at their Fourth of July party.

In front of her mom and dad, Ellie, and pretty much all their guests.

Darian had let Jayne know the producer had the smallest pecker he'd ever seen.

"Gen, Jayne, take a seat." He got up and came around the desk. In her mind, the words *smallest pecker, smallest pecker, smallest pecker* were skipping around like a broken record.

He sat on the edge of the desk as Jayne and her mom sat on the chairs in front of him. He must've been her mom's age, but he looked much younger with those chipmunk cheeks of his.

Jayne turned to try to read her mom's face. Gen was staring straight ahead and had her newscaster smile on, her hands folded over her crossed knees.

This wasn't going to be good.

"So, Jayne, your mom and I have been talking and came up with something that we think you'll be excited about."

Unless it had something to do with a paid trip to Italy, she doubted that whatever was about to come out of his mouth was going to be good.

"There are millions of teenage girls like you, Jayne. Pretty, smart." He paused and hummed, like he was trying to find the right word. "Directionless."

Jayne now knew what a trapped animal felt like.

"Gen and I have been brainstorming, and we think it's time to sit down and discuss The Thompkins Tragedy."

Jayne still felt paralyzed, and no words came to her. No words except for the dazed response of, "I'm already going to Larry the Fairy."

"What?"

Jayne looked at her mom, who was still wearing that Stepford-like smile.

"Are you trying to be our family counselor?" Jayne asked.

Cameron laughed. The boyish giggle grated on her for the thirty or so seconds he shook and his face turned red. When he caught his breath, he wiped his eyes. "That was priceless. No, I meant you and your mom should sit down in front of the cameras. Discuss what happened."

Jayne didn't say anything. She was not comprehending a thing.

"Jayne, what Cameron is attempting to say is he wants you to come on my Saturday show," Gen said, her words crisp and precise. "The whole hour. Just you and me and The Thompkins Tragedy."

Suddenly the situation became very clear.

"Are you friggin' kidding me?"

"Dead serious, Jayne. You're out of control. I think this sit-down will help."

"Help? Help who?"

Then it became crystal clear. "What, Mom," she mocked, "are your ratings down?"

Then something happened that Jayne had never seen in her whole life: Her mother blushed.

Cameron started talking again, but he was looking at her mom. "We want you to share your story. Girls your age want to know your story. Like that girl who was at your folks' party the other night . . . Lori, I think? Lori told me she'd love to see you on TV, talking about what happened." He put his hands in the air, forming a box. "Picture it. We'd have you go back to that day when you hit Brenda Deavers—"

Jayne stared at his mouth and tried to process his words. Or were these her mother's words? She glanced at Gen.

Her hands were folded, her eyes averted.

"—and of course there'd be a psychologist there to help with the interview. You know, discuss what the psychological toll is, what a person goes through after such a horrible happenstance, how a person can get over it."

This guy was certifiable. And her mom? Her mother finally looked at her.

And had the gall not to look embarrassed in the least.

Jayne was no longer Gen's daughter at this moment. No, she was a story that could help Gen move from the small time to . . . to . . . whatever Oprah was considered.

"Excuse me." Jayne interrupted Cameron as he went into something about beating the other networks at the ratings game.

"Yes, Jayne? Ask me any questions. We're here to make this experience as smooth as possible for you."

Jayne smiled. Well, her lips smiled, but that was only to keep them busy so she wasn't tempted to call this guy a gutless worm in front of her mom. Actually . . . "First of all, Cameron, you're high on crack if you think the idea you have here is a good one."

"Not a good one?" He sounded confused, like he'd never considered the possibility of Gen Thompkins's daughter saying no. Funny how he'd ignored the "high on crack" comment.

"No." Jayne's voice was low and her hands were curled around the edge of her denim skirt. Her stomach was a hailstorm of acid right now. "Not now, not ever."

"Jayne, take a moment and consider this opportunity. It could count toward your counseling hours."

Jayne didn't say anything. The inane comment didn't deserve a reply.

She turned to look at her mom again. She had her cool-and-collected-journalist face on. Like Jayne wasn't even her daughter.

"It'll be like when you and Ellie were little and did those commercials for the station." Her mom's voice had taken on the quality of "Remember the happy times?"

"This is not the same thing, Mother." Those commercials had been of her and Ellie riding a covered wagon with their mom advertising Channel 16 as the "Best in the West."

And both she and Ellie had fallen into scorpion weed and had a burning rash for two weeks.

Yeah, fun times.

"It's either this or we're tripling your sessions with Larry." Her mother really could've been a ventriloquist. Her lips had barely moved as she offered the ultimatum.

An ultimatum? The way Jayne saw it, she could either be humiliated in front of a live studio audience or have her mom spend even more money a week to have Larry water and Jayne read.

She knew a no-brainer when she saw one. "I'll take Larry."

The expression on her mom's face told Jayne she had made the wrong choice.

"I see here that maybe some more thought needs to go into this. Cool beans." Cameron rubbed his hands together. "I'll just line up that dog trainer instead, Gen, the one who works with those Westminster dogs. Sound like a plan?"

Gen didn't take her eyes off of her daughter. "Sounds fine, Cameron."

He picked up his phone. "So, if we're done here, I better get on the horn, line up that trainer. Hopefully she can make it this Saturday, it being such short notice."

This Saturday? Her mom had wanted her to do this next weekend? Jayne felt her face grow red. Her mom must've noticed, because her expressionless newscaster mask was slipping a little. Jayne thought she might've even seen a little bit of uncertainty in Emmy-winning but ratings-loser Gen Thompkins's eyes.

Jayne got up and left. A bus stop was just three blocks from here.

She was propelled by disgust and . . . yep, rage. *So this is what rage feels like.*

Like her stomach had a pot of water boiling in it.

Water that was beginning to boil over.

It was only twelve-thirty in the afternoon, but it was already pushing 110 degrees.

Jayne closed her eyes. Her mother had ambushed her.

And she wasn't the least bit remorseful.

She tried to calm herself down. She visualized Gen sitting in one of her thousand-dollar suits interviewing a dog trainer. Trying to keep her smile in place and the look of disgust off her face for following a story that was beneath her.

Gen wasn't big into what she considered unsuccessful people.

Jayne had always known that. But for the first time, she was really seeing it.

She opened her eyes and tried to forget about the whole horrible experience. But it was hard. Especially since she was in yet another horrible situation, sitting at a bus stop with a lady who reeked of stale garlic and too much rose perfume.

She was trying to see how long she could hold her breath when she heard a squeal of tires. She looked up.

And saw Darian in his BMW, the passenger-side window rolled down. "Hey there, stranger. Want a ride?"

Her heart did a double flip. His being here was surreal.

His grin was big and inviting. "Just came from renewing my vehicle registration and I need something to wash away the taste of the DMV. Wanna get a shake?"

Jayne grabbed her bag, every fiber of her body humming. Then she saw the little old lady was waving her over.

"Honey, I'm taking down his license plate in case anything happens to you."

For the first time in recent memory, Jayne laughed. Out loud.

And for real.

23

JAYNE DIDN'T GO HOME. She had Darian take her to Outreach Arizona. She beelined it to Meadow, telling her that she needed her help. When the bored rich girl had heard about the plan, she'd gotten on board.

"What color are we going for here? Cookie Monster blue? Bubbleicious pink?"

"Brown."

The girl with the orange mohawk and shredded Lindsay Lohan T-shirt smirked at Jayne.

"Aren't you quite the daredevil."

"C'mon, Jayne, get a little wild." Meadow sat on the velvet sofa in the center of the black-on-black salon, her eyes meeting Jayne's in the mirror. "I brought you to Destiny because she's great at Technicolor."

Jayne didn't need wild. She needed shock factor. Especially after today, when her mom sprang that little ambush on her. She needed something Gen Thompkins would swallow her tongue over. That's why she was letting a girl with more holes in her than a golf course stand over her with a straight razor and a smile.

That's why she wasn't with Gustav, her mother's colorist. The guy who'd made her a blonde at age thirteen and every eight weeks thereafter.

Just thinking about it made the rage burn bright, white-hot. What kind of mother would cajole her pubescent daughter to burn her scalp with peroxide?

The same woman who'd told Jayne, "You'll be prettier, and prettier is always better in this world we live in."

Jayne scrutinized herself in the round mirror. "I'm going with plain brown. That's my natural color, anyway."

Destiny ran her fingers through Jayne's long, silky strands. "We're keeping the length, right?"

Jayne suddenly felt like little fairies were making flowers grow in her stomach. She was *that* excited. "Nope. Chop it."

Destiny's mouth opened, showing the silver barbell piercing the flesh of her tongue. "We're not talking *G.I. Jane* buzz cut, right? 'Cause I don't do ugly."

"No." Jayne pulled her hair back so that the only hair that was showing was what was left on the top and sides. "Short like Charlize Theron will do."

Destiny ran her hands down the sides of Jayne's hair, her head cocked to one side. A tiny silver skull dangled from the six-inch chain pierced to her ear. "I can see that on you. You've got the bones to pull off something like that." She put her hands on Jayne's shoulders, her eyes growing serious behind her cat-eye rhinestone-studded glasses. "I know you're messing with your hair to piss someone off, but can I at least suggest some red highlights? Your hair will still have the piss-off factor but it will also have some style."

Jayne studied her face in the mirror, imagining her new bi-colored hair standing up all over the place. Like some starving artist type living off Top Ramen and canned peaches.

Her mom would die.

"Go for it."

"What's next?" Meadow slurped at a mocha double-whipped something-or-other as she edged her Mercedes convertible out of the parking lot.

Jayne stared at the face looking back at her from the sideview mirror. Her body was on edge, like it wanted her to do something else.

Something nuts.

Jayne couldn't have agreed more.

"Do you know where the closest sanitary piercing parlor is around here?"

Meadow's cool blue eyes took Jayne in. She flipped on the air conditioner full blast while she pushed a button to roll down all four windows. In a bored voice she asked, "What, are you going to be a daredevil and get two holes in each ear? As much fun as that sounds, I've gotta get going." She sucked noisily on the straw. "I'm meeting my personal trainer later."

It looked like Meadow was done with today's portion of "See Jayne Get a Makeover."

"I'm thinking of getting a barbell." Jayne paused, mulling over the words before she said them. "Like the one Destiny had."

"In your tongue?" Meadow took her eyes off the traffic. Based on the glossy lips forming a glistening O, it looked like an afternoon filled with three sets of eight was just going to have to wait.

Jayne settled back in the seat and her eyes fell on a boy staring at her from the back of a rusted car with Mexico license plates. He waved at her enthusiastically. She winked back at him.

Where had that come from? She'd never winked at anyone in her life, much less a strange boy in a beat-up car. She sat back and let the warm wind whip her face. It felt pretty good. Empowering, even, to interact with another human being.

She'd never really gotten this high from a test before. Or from keeping her spot on the tennis team.

Adrenaline, maybe, from the stress. But never an out-of-body happiness.

Jayne felt her stomach do a tiny flip-flop. She closed her eyes and enjoyed this feeling of . . . weightlessness.

24

JAYNE EASED the front door shut, wincing as her shirt stretched across her stomach. Canned laughter of some studio audience floated to her as she slipped off her shoes. She winced yet again as her stomach rubbed the waistband of her jeans.

The clink of a piece of ice hitting against crystal came from the dark study to her left. "God, Jayne. What have you done?"

Ellie leaned against the doorjamb, her hand wrapped around a squat glass holding some kind of liquid. Her other hand held a cigarette.

Jayne wondered briefly if the Lobotomy Fairy had dropped by when she was out.

Jayne slammed her eyes shut, hoping that when she opened them again, Ellie was just a pain-induced mirage. She opened her eyes.

Crap.

"Have you lost your mind? Dad's going to smell that smoke as soon as he walks through the door. You know how sensitive he is to that kind of stuff."

Her sister shrugged, the knot of hair on top of her head bouncing with the effort. "Like I give a rat's fart."

Jayne raised an eyebrow. Ellie liked pushing the envelope with their folks. But this was suicidal.

Ellie rolled her eyes. "Dad's gone. An emergency marketing meeting about some lotion turning people's skin green or something. And Mom won't care."

It wasn't so much that their mother wouldn't care. It was mainly that Gen Thompkins, the woman who ate a macrobiotic diet and did cardio seven days a week, would be puffing away on her own stash of cigarettes before her health-fanatic hubby got home.

She would think the smoke smell was her own smoke.

Ellie punched her cigarette in Jayne's direction. "What's up with the make-under?"

Jayne smoothed a hand down the back of her head. "I like to think of it as going back to my roots. *Our* roots."

Ellie perused her with half-hooded eyes. It seemed like she wanted to say something. She opened her mouth. After a minute, she exhaled and closed her mouth. Shrugged. "Whatever. I don't care."

She sipped from the glass and grimaced. Jayne knew she cared. The only reason Ellie had gone blonde was that Jayne had.

Jayne remembered that day. She'd held her then eleven-year-old sister's hand while the bleach sat in her brown hair, burning into her scalp for an hour.

She took in Ellie, with her glass of alcohol and boredom written all over her. "So, wanna help me test-drive this hair?"

Ellie's eyes brightened for a second. But then that guarded look came into them again.

"You can't drive and I'm not taking the bus."

"Fine." Hearing Ellie talk about one of the stipulations of her probation didn't send the usual dart of pain to her stomach. Instead, Jayne moved to stand beside Ellie and put an arm around her shoulders. She plucked the cigarette out of her fingers, examined the burning tip, and took a drag.

It looked like she wasn't done being bad quite yet.

"You're forgetting, Elle, that I've got friends in high places. With nice cars. With enough room for two girls looking for some fun."

"Yeah?" Jayne felt the tension ease out of Ellie's shoulders with the word.

"Yeah." Jayne dropped the cigarette in Ellie's still-full glass. The soggy ciggy was done for the night. "So scrub the stink off your teeth while I make a call."

Ellie squealed in her ear. "Are we, like, going *out* out?"

"Sure." It was Jayne's turn to shrug. "Why not?"

"Like to a party?"

"Yep."

"With boys?"

"There'll probably be some."

"And a keg?"

"If the boys have their way, yeah."

Ellie threw her arms around Jayne, squeezing her so tight that Ellie's hipbone hit Jayne's stomach.

Jayne let out a low hiss between her clenched teeth.

"What's up, Jaynie?"

Jaynie rubbed her stomach through the thin cotton of her black tank top. "I didn't just get my hair cut today."

Jayne tugged the fabric away from the angry red skin.

"Oh. My. God!" Ellie shrieked the words as she bent to inspect the barbell piercing the top portion of Jayne's belly button. "You didn't!"

She flicked the tiny rhinestone star hanging from the end of it.

"Hey!" Jayne jerked out of Ellie's reach.

"I can't believe you got a belly-button ring before I did. It looks awesome." She started dragging Jayne with her down the hall, the glass of whiskey and drowned cigarette left behind on the foyer table. "C'mon, you gotta wear those jeans I got you two Christmases ago. People've gotta see this."

"There's a reason I've never worn them." They showed butt crack. Jayne wasn't a butt crack kind of girl. "And there's no way you're going to get me in them."

Jayne felt behind her again, her fingers gliding over her lower back.

No butt crack was showing.

However, her belly ring was being shown off in all its newly pierced glory.

She slammed the BMW's door shut, trying to pull her black tank top down. Trying to cover up her three inches of bare tummy.

Each time she pulled the fabric down, it just shot right back up again.

She'd once been a girl who'd tied a sweatshirt around her

waist in the middle of summer to keep her too-short top from crawling up all day. She hadn't taken it off once.

And it had been 112 degrees that day. And her waist had been pouring sweat.

"Where are we going again?" Ellie's shoulder brushed against hers as she click-clacked across the parking lot in a pair of four-inch heels that made her legs longer and leaner.

She was wearing her do-me shoes. They'd once been their mom's, but Ellie had inherited them after her mom had declared them dated.

When Jayne had seen Ellie in her short jean skirt and sky-high heels, it had taken everything within Jayne's power to bite back the words *Go change*.

Ellie was Ellie. Jayne was Jayne.

They were both big girls.

They were both capable of taking care of themselves.

"We're going to a friend's houseboat." Darian came around the car and slipped an arm around Jayne's waist. "Can't wait to show you off, you wild girl, you."

She looked up and saw his eyes matching the teasing tone in his words.

"You don't think I went overboard?" Jayne had started feeling like the old, cautious, overthinking Jayne about half an hour ago, when Darian had picked them up and greeted her with "Holy mother of Jesus!"

She felt his fingers fluff the back of her hair. Her skin tingled from the caress. He whispered close to her ear, "I think you look hot, Jayne Thompkins. Totally hot."

Jayne felt a blush heat her cheeks, but she silently reveled in his words.

"Are we gonna, like, fish?"

Darian laughed, his body shaking against Jayne's. It felt nice. Natural.

It was friggin' great.

"This isn't exactly a fishing expedition." Jayne watched Darian's face while he talked. There was just enough moonlight for her to make out that gorgeous jock-boy face of his. "Derek's got three flat screens, a pool table, something like ten Jet Skis."

"Really?" Ellie sounded disappointed, judging by the level of whine in her voice. "I didn't bring a suit."

"That's okay." He pulled Jayne closer as the three of them navigated the steep hill leading from the parking lot to the docks on Lake Pleasant. They were about thirty miles outside of Phoenix, where a lot of the city went to remember what water looked like. "You can strip down to underwear here, or skin. It's that kind of crowd."

Ellie moved in front of them, walking backward. Jayne admired the way she didn't biff it in those heels.

"Jaynie, I think I'm liking this new crowd of yours."

Ellie skipped ahead. This was the happiest Jayne had seen her sister in weeks. Heck, this was the happiest Jayne had *felt* in months.

Ahead of them was the one lone restaurant the lake had. It was one of those places that turned into a bar at night and had a dress code of swimsuits, sunburns, and day-old suntan lotion. Jayne had been here before, when her mom and dad had taken her to a party on one of the huge houseboats parked at these docks.

She didn't feel like some sixteen-year-old, though. Not with this hair, this piercing, these jeans.

This boy.

"Hey, Darian."

"Hey, Jayne."

"You've got fake ID, right? You seem like the type of guy who would."

Darian laughed, tightening his arm around her. "Yeah, why?"

Jayne leaned closer, resting her head on his chest. "I'm thinking a six-pack or two."

"Of Diet Pepsi?"

She pulled away. She saw the teasing in his eyes. "Sure. If that's what they're calling Heineken nowadays."

25

"WHERE WERE YOU TWO last night?" Sean Thompkins looked over his reading glasses, taking in the scene in front of him. "Having fun, I hope?"

Jayne was too tired to answer. She rested her forehead on her hand and wrapped her other one around her orange juice. Heineken needed a warning label. Not for pregnant people. For teenage people who'd never drunk before.

Warning: Drinking a beer and a half might make you throw up three times. And miss the toilet one of those times.

"I think I had more fun than Jaynie here." Ellie pulled apart a cinnamon bun, popping the center into her mouth. Her parents didn't say anything about Ellie's sugar-filled food choice. She wouldn't, either. "She's not used to . . . um . . . fun."

Gen Thompkins flipped through a tabloid. She hadn't said good morning when they sat down. She had, however, pushed *Star* over to Ellie, since she liked looking at the Best and Worst Dressed.

She still hadn't acknowledged Jayne.

The phone ringing interrupted Jayne's thoughts.

"Gen Thompkins here." Her mom always answered the phone that way. Like she was taking a call in her office or something. "Yes, she's here. Just a moment, please."

She put the phone down in front of Jayne and sat back down.

I guess it's for me.

Jayne took the cordless and walked to the living room.

"Hey."

It was Darian.

"Hey yourself."

"You're coming to Outreach later, right?" he asked.

"Last time I checked, I still have a court order to appear." Had she just attempted a joke about her probation?

That was a first. Having a hangover and downing six aspirins must've loosened her up a bit.

"Just making sure." He dropped his voice. "I've got something for you."

"Yeah?"

"Yeah. And you'll be knocking yourself out trying to think of ways to thank me."

"Why do you say that?" He had a present for her? Why'd he have a present? It wasn't her birthday. Heck, they weren't even seeing each other.

Yet.

"You'll see."

They both hung up a few minutes later, with Jayne still not knowing what Darian had for her.

The surprise of not knowing was kind of nice. It gave her butterflies that felt sort of good.

"What's the deal with this boy?"

Gen stood behind her, her arms crossed, a magazine in one hand, open and hanging to the side.

"There's no *deal*, Mother."

"From what I've seen, I beg to differ."

Jayne walked back to the kitchen and hung up the phone. Her dad was still there, doing the newspaper's crossword. Ellie was gone. Probably upstairs sleeping some more.

"He was asking if I'd be at the Outreach program today."

"How are things going there, kiddo?" Her dad looked up from his crossword, his eyes moving from Jayne to Gen and back again. "You doing okay?"

She knew that she had to answer this question carefully. Otherwise she'd be getting another session with Larry tacked on. "Yeah. Answering phones isn't that hard."

"Get any interesting calls over there?"

She shook her head, watching as her mom focused on the tabloid she'd been carrying around. She was pretending like she wasn't listening to the conversation. But Jayne knew her mother's routine—turn the pages fast and furious, tearing out any stories that interested her: five-year-old beauty queens, dogs that could bark "The Star-Spangled Banner."

She'd been on the same page now for at least a minute.

"I haven't been trained yet. Maria said maybe in a month."

"Sounds good, kid. Glad that you have something to do this summer."

"She has *school*." Gen's words sounded strangled. "That should be all she's concentrating on."

Jayne grabbed a water from the fridge. Her mother was right. She should be concentrating on Arizona history.

Too bad she wasn't. And too bad she had a C-minus in there right now.

The third week of a five-week class.

"I better go take a shower. See you, Dad."

She was through the door and halfway down the hall when she heard her mother's voice. Purposely loud and clear.

"She looks like a lesbian, Sean. That gorgeous hair has been chopped. Ruined."

Jayne smiled.

This day just kept getting better and better.

The day had just gotten worse.

"Is this Jayne?"

"Yeah?" The word came out while she tried to catch her breath. She'd just finished one hundred crunches, and her stomach felt like she'd done one thousand. God, she was friggin' out of shape.

"Val here. Val Shetland. I didn't catch you at a bad time, did I?"

Jayne didn't just have trouble breathing. She forgot to breathe. What did her lawyer want? "Nuh-uh."

"I got a call from one of the driver's lawyers today. The one with the black Mercedes. The jerk wasn't even hurt and he wants to sue for monetary damages."

"Why's he suing us?" The words weren't computing.

"He says it's because of recurring back pain that's kept him from making his full salary for the last couple of months. I say it's because he saw your mom on her billboard down on Central and decided big billboard means big bucks."

Jayne kept hearing Val explaining the situation, but the

answer wasn't making sense. "But doesn't he have money, this Mercedes guy?"

"Apparently not enough." Val snorted. "Some people have really huge *cojones*, you know?"

Jayne dropped back, lying full-length on the mat. She stared at the high wood beams above her. What was this guy's problem? It'd been two months. Two months with nothing. "Why now?"

"Who knows. Maybe a wife who needs a nose job, or a new plasma TV is on the market. Whatever. His lawyer says it's because he didn't associate the back pain with the accident. I still say he didn't make the link until he saw the ten-foot reminder on Central that he had a savings account to cash in on."

"Have you called my mom or dad yet?"

Her dad was at a book-signing in downtown Phoenix. A high school buddy had a new mystery out. Gen was meeting with an alpaca rancher on the outskirts of town, directing the background shots for her story.

"No. You're my first call. The most important part of this equation."

Jayne wished she was an important part of a *different* equation. This one sucked.

"Are you—I mean, are we giving him any money?"

"Some. His lawyer's asking for fifty thousand dollars for lost time at work, chiropractor bills, and pain and suffering."

"How about his car?"

"Your auto insurance took care of that."

She didn't want to, but she asked the question anyway. "How about Mrs. Deavers? Is she filing anything?"

"Nope. Nothing yet. I don't think she will, though."

Jayne concentrated on the beams above her. One had a loose spiderweb floating from it. "Why do you think that? Did she tell you that?"

Please oh please oh please.

"No, she didn't tell me anything. But she let her kid ride in the front seat of her car, without a seat belt on. The seat where the kid got slammed in the face with an air bag. An air bag that has the same force behind it as a twelve-gauge shotgun, mind you." Val said something to someone on her side of the phone, the words a murmur and unintelligible.

"But she can still blame me, right?" And take her parents' money. A lot of money—money that a ten-foot sign on Central was advertising for anybody to see.

"Honey, I don't think you need to worry about taking full blame. Mrs. Deavers is just as at fault as you are."

26

mrs. deavers *is just as at fault as you are.*

The sentence replayed in her head over and over again.

Jayne looked at the clock. 3:32 A.M.

She'd been stealing looks at the stupid thing since 1:01. Val's call was keeping her up. The blowup fight she'd had with her mother, whom Val had called right after, was keeping her up.

The words "If you hadn't been so careless, Jayne, none of this would've happened. None of this!" completed the cycle playing in her head.

Mrs. Deavers is just as at fault as you are.

If you hadn't been so careless, Jayne, none of this would've happened. None of this!

Mrs. Deavers is just as at fault as you are.

If you hadn't been so careless, Jayne, none of this would've happened. . . .

She flipped on her computer. She wanted to do something, but what?

She drummed her fingers lightly on top of the keys.

What to do. What to do . . .

The answer, when it came, was obvious. And simple. And Jayne wondered why she'd never done it before.

She typed in:

AIR BAG CHILD DEATH

For the next hour and a half, she read.

And read.

And read.

"You have the Deaverses' address?"

Tom hadn't even had the chance to knock on the front door. She'd yanked it open as soon as she saw him walking down the street.

Jayne was antsy. Antsy to get this done and over with.

And Tom was here to give her that courage.

He handed her a piece of paper, his hair still mussed from sleeping. "Yeah. They were in the phone book."

"I looked in the phone book. I didn't see them."

"They were under another name. She was under her first married name, before she remarried and had Brenda."

They went upstairs, and Jayne closed the door behind her. Her dad was on his run and her mom was on the treadmill downstairs, oblivious to the world for the next hour and a half. But Jayne didn't want them to know Tom was there.

The Thompkinses' position on boys in their daughters' bedrooms held for Tom, too. He'd been there when Charlie Monteague was caught in Ellie's room. Gen had called the cops and the boy's parents.

And no one at Palm Desert had seen Charlie since.

Tom was always in Jayne's room and hadn't been caught yet.

The eucalyptus tree outside was sturdy and well-worn, thanks to years as Tom's quick getaway route to his house two streets over.

Right now, Tom was giving her a weird look, his "How do I put this" look. Jayne's stomach dipped a little. Those long curly eyelashes of his definitely gave him the edge as far as looks went. Usually, if he stayed quiet long enough and just gazed at her with minimal blinking, she'd spill her guts to him.

But telling him that she was about to write a letter to Mrs. Donna Deavers calling her an idiot wasn't going to go over well with Tom. He and his stupid nice-boy tendencies would talk her out of it.

Instead, she'd told him she was writing Mrs. Deavers an apology note.

He hadn't thought that was a very good idea, either. "You know that if you send a letter, she'll have in writing you admitting you killed her daughter."

Jayne did know. Val had warned her about writing anything. Both at her sentencing and when she'd called about the black Mercedes guy.

"No worries, Tom." Darian's "no worries" thing pretty much summed up how she was approaching life at the moment. She had too many worries to give them any kind of proper attention anymore. Why not forget them all? "I'm not going to tell her I aimed my car at hers so I'd push them into oncoming traffic."

She attempted a smile to acknowledge the morbid humor. "I'm not that good a driver."

But she wasn't writing to Mrs. Deavers to admit she was to

blame for that little girl's death. She was writing to blame Mrs. Deavers.

Brenda Deavers had been killed by her mom and her stupidity. She'd died because Donna Deavers hadn't been one of the ninety-nine percent of parents who were aware that kids shouldn't be put in the front seat of a car with an air bag.

Her Google search had told her that.

Brenda Deavers had also not been wearing a seat belt. Between no seat belt and the air bag's impact, the kid didn't have a chance.

Another Googled bit of information.

And maybe if she'd been wearing that seat belt in the backseat, Brenda would still be alive and the Deavers would just have a totaled car.

"I know what I'm doing, Tom." She turned to the computer.

She started typing in the address she'd copied onto a Post-it. She heard a noise behind her and glanced around. Tom must've rolled closer to her, because his face seemed an awful lot closer than it had been. "Do you need something?" she asked.

He opened his mouth and closed it. He opened his mouth again. And closed it. Finally, he said, "You know you're important to me, right?"

She nodded. Her fingers over the keyboard slowed to a halt.

"So write this letter. Don't write this letter. It doesn't matter. Whatever makes you get . . . get over this? Do it."

Get over this. Was there such a thing?

He said that now. But what was he going to say when he found out she'd told Donna Deavers she was an idiot? Tom would think she was insane.

She saw his eyes shift to her lips.

Jayne's stomach dipped.

"What's going on, Tom?" A tiny voice in the back of her head was whispering something. *Kiss me.*

"I . . ." He cleared his throat. "I want the old Jayne back."

Kiss me.

"Yeah?"

Kiss me.

The front door slammed.

Without a word, Tom shot up and made his way to the window and the tree outside.

27

SHE PICKED ANOTHER ONION out of her pasta. She'd asked for no onions. But she'd gotten onions anyway.

Story of her life.

"Jayne."

She heard her mom's whisper. She also felt her mom's fake nails digging into her leg. But she ignored her and her nails and her tone of voice.

Whatever her mom was going to say wasn't going to make her feel better.

"So, Harry." Her dad balanced a piece of his vegetarian lasagna on his fork. "You have a pretty nice ride out there. I take it it's the new one?"

"Yes, had the dealership put me first on their waiting list. Just got it." The tall, thin man rubbed his hands together and leaned across the table. His oval eyeglasses picked up the candle flicker in the middle of the table, making him look possessed. "And man, what a dream."

What a douche.

The tall, thin man was Harry Stansfield, the mystery writer

Jayne's dad had gone to high school with. He'd written twenty books in fifteen years, all self-published. And, according to her mom, all awful.

All he'd been talking about for the last hour was his new house, his new car, and his new born-rich wife with her new boobs. (The "new boobs" part Jayne figured out from the picture he showed everyone.)

Her parents had invited her along because Harry Stansfield was also a Harvard alumnus.

Based on what she'd seen so far, this guy definitely wasn't the best PR for Harvard.

"Jayne."

The whisper was more urgent. And pissed-off-sounding. Her dad and Harry were too busy talking about Harry to hear Gen.

"What." Jayne looked up, her word a statement more than her wondering or caring what it was her mom wanted. Gen sat ramrod straight, a teeny-tiny salad she hadn't touched in front of her.

"Stop using your fingers. You look like an animal."

Jayne stared at her mom, her thumb and forefinger about to go in for another slimy onion. Without breaking her gaze, she reached in, dug around, and found another one. She yanked it out victoriously, set it on her bread plate, and went back for more.

"Then don't watch me."

"I hear you're Harvard-bound, young lady."

Dinner was over. Harry was drinking a mixture of scotch and whatever, her dad had gone to the restroom, and her mom was chatting with some slightly drunk people at the next table who'd bribed her into sharing a martini with them when they found out she really was *the* Gen Thompkins.

"That was the plan." Jayne was resting her forehead on her icy water glass. Phoenix summer nights were still warmer than most people's summer days.

"Harvard was great. It opened a lot of doors, I can tell you that."

Her parents were otherwise occupied, so that meant she had to play the hostess. It was too ingrained in her to do otherwise.

"You wrote twenty books, right?"

"Yeah." He leaned back, his cheek on his hand. A slight smile on his face, like he was proud of himself.

"With all those Harvard contacts and all, why did you have to self-publish your books?"

Some of that smile eased away. So much for the compliment he thought he was going to get. "No one hits big with their first book unless they're like J. K. Rowling with that Harry Potter of hers."

He took a sip of his drink, his lips thin and sort of uptight-looking. "Anyway, I'll make it one day. I'm a Harvard graduate, for God's sake. Even got a partial scholarship for a while." He winked at her. Jayne's skin crawled. "Ended up with a 2.9 GPA, which wasn't that stellar, but for a guy with an allergy against all things math, that was pretty dang good."

Uh-huh. Sure. "So, Harry." She leaned closer. Maybe it was the hot night, maybe it was her mom being her anal-retentive self. Whatever it was, she felt a little reckless. "How do you think you got into Harvard?"

He looked like he wasn't sure if she was insulting him or just inquisitive. Jayne didn't know herself. "Good GPA. Good extra-curriculars. But I think my essay really stood out. You know, where you discuss why you deserve to be there and who your heroes are and all that kind of bull crap?"

Jayne, for the first time that night, was interested in this guy. "What did you write yours about?"

Harry had a far-off look in his eyes, a silly smile on his face. "To write the great American novel, since, in my opinion, it hadn't been written yet." He lifted his glass to Jayne. "Here's to the great American novel I have yet to write."

Jayne lifted her water glass and clinked glasses. In her own head, she toasted, *If this putz can get into Harvard, I can, too.*

28

YOU SEND THAT LETTER YET?" Tom tied his shoe-lace, like the answer didn't matter. Jayne knew him better than that.

Jayne shook her head and popped open her soda. "I want to proofread it one more time. Probably later in the week."

There were only about five more minutes of break left. Mr. Munroe hadn't gotten any more interesting in four weeks. Jayne had to drink two Diet Pepsis every morning just to get through the class.

At least she was in B territory with her grade.

And after that talk with that Harvard idiot, she'd asked Mr. Munroe to help her get extra credit in order to boost her grade. He'd assigned her a five-thousand-word essay on the four C's of Arizona.

Bor-ing. But at least an A was in sight.

Tom ate the last Cheeto in his bag and balled up the plastic and shot it into the trash can by Mr. Munroe's desk. The move reminded her of Darian.

Somehow, her heart didn't beat so fast thinking about

Darian. Not like it did with Tom, who was currently keeping at least two feet between them at all times.

Jayne hated the weird vibe. Then again, she kind of liked this new electricity between them.

She didn't know what any of it meant. She kind of didn't want to know.

"I'm glad you haven't sent it. Without proofreading it, I mean." He scooted his notebook around on his desk, concentrating on lining up the edges of the desk.

"You know, I—"

"Tom!" Lori stood outside the doorway, beckoning Tom with a hand.

The words she was going to say, *I was thinking that I shouldn't send it,* died on her lips. Tom looked at Jayne, then back at Lori. "Hey, Lori."

"Tom, come here."

"I'll catch up with you later, Lori."

Tom, his back to Lori, mouthed, "She's stalking me."

"Sure." Jayne thought about the blog, the eggings, her locker. She hadn't really talked to Tom about any of it, though.

That would constitute her talking about, well, the accident.

Which meant that he probably thought Lori wasn't the spawn of Satan. That Lori had spared Jayne in her terrorization of the rest of the Palm Desert population.

That she was really a very nice girl underneath it all.

"Honest, Jayne. We talked at your house on the Fourth of July, but I don't hang out with her."

She looked for the eye twitch. Her personal lie detector. Nothing.

"We say hi in school, but that's about it."

It looked like his left eye twitched a little. Then again, it could've been an eyelash.

She gave him a tight smile. "Sure thing. No worries."

Behind him, Lori hadn't moved. She stood in the hallway, both middle fingers flipping Jayne off.

"Where would you like it, hon?"

"On my back, below my waist, above my butt crack."

Jayne was at the 7th Street Tattoo Palace, the most hygienic parlor in the city. She'd picked out her design. She had also already taken two Advil.

The heavyset woman with tattoos down her arms, across her chest, and up her neck held the needle in her hand. "And you're eighteen, hon?"

"Sure am." The lie rolled off her tongue. This place was also known for inking teenagers without parental consent.

"And you're sure?"

"Yep."

The woman started to transfer the design onto Jayne's skin. When the needle punctured her skin minutes later, thoughts of her mother, the Harvard guy, the guy suing her parents, the letter to Mrs. Deavers, Tom's eye twitch, and Lori's hateful face disappeared.

Pain had a way of doing that.

Jayne rotated her wrist. The Swarovski crystals twinkled under the Outreach program's fluorescent lights. "I can't take this."

Even as she said the words, she knew they were the ones her

parents raised her to say. What she actually wanted to say was, *I love it and I never want to take it off.*

It definitely was taking her mind off being sued. That was one powerful bracelet.

"I'm not taking it back." Darian hooked his hands behind his head, his legs stretched out in front of him on one of Outreach's coffee tables. "And if you put it on the table, I'm just going to leave it there. Maybe the janitor will pick it up."

The bracelet sparkled, picking up any and all rays of light. God, it was gorgeous. And it was her first gift ever from a boy, minus the presents from her dad and Tom.

The nicest thing she'd ever gotten Tom was a book of Herb Ritts pictures. That'd been a great gift. The most Jayne-like gift ever.

But this one was three strands of clear and light topaz crystals, a present she never would've spent money on for herself. Her mom had one almost exactly like it and had picked it up after landing an interview with a reclusive rocker in the West Valley.

Jayne'd seen her mom's Nordstrom receipt. For something that looked like it'd come from Claire's Accessories and had been neighbors with $3.95 rhinestone hairclips, the $750 price tag had caused a shock to the system.

And now she had one.

"Okay then." She looked around them, where cubicles were filled with people talking on the phone or to one another. In a lower voice, she asked, "Why exactly are you giving this to me?"

"Why not?"

Jayne gave him a look that let him know he was full of it.

"Maybe it's because I got it cheap. Maybe it's because I think you're pretty cool." He leaned closer. "Maybe it's because I want to molest you later."

Jayne pulled away so fast, her head hit his chin and she saw white pinpricks of light for a second.

"Darian, I . . ."

"I'm joking, Jaynie." He put a finger on the bracelet before running it up her arm. She shivered. She didn't know if it was because of how cold it was in here.

Or if it was a momentary case of the heebie-jeebies about Darian telling her he wanted to molest her.

"No worries, okay?" He pulled her close, ignoring the half-filled cubicles around them.

Across the building, she saw Maria glance their way, tap her watch, and go into her office. Jayne met Darian's eyes, looking for the lie. She was sick of being lied to. "No strings?"

He squeezed her closer. "No strings."

29

YOU AND DARIAN are getting pretty close, huh?"

Meadow's words were muffled as she pulled the lace-trimmed shirt over her head. Jayne had just finished pulling on a long-sleeved black shirt, a black dragon embossed on the front in velvet. After they'd finished up with Outreach for the day, Meadow thought it was time to go on to step two of Makeover Jayne: clothes.

And now they were sharing the same changing room in a trendy little shop that had just opened in the Paradise Valley mall.

The old Jayne would've wanted to be alone in her own room, with periodic check-ins in the hallway. The tattooed, pierced Jayne? She didn't give a crap.

Much.

"Yeah. We're getting to know each other a lot more."

"A *lot* more?" Meadow's eyebrows went up and down and her mouth twisted into a smirk. Meadow liked her smirks, that was for sure.

Jayne knew what that smirk meant, too. "No, not like that. I mean we're having fun."

"Like fun as in naked parts pressed against other naked parts?"

"No!" Jayne laughed and pulled on the black skirt she'd brought in. "No naked parts are being pressed together."

"Yet." Meadow wiggled into a pair of tight jeans. "By the way, that shirt looks awesome with your hair."

Jayne fluffed her hair in the mirror and didn't say anything. She didn't correct Meadow or go into details. She didn't even know where this thing with Darian was going. And she definitely wasn't going to hypothesize where this thing was going with one of his closest friends.

A half hour later, they went to the cashier, an armload of clothes in their arms.

"I'm sorry, but this card doesn't work." The tiny Latina girl behind the register held Jayne's credit card out to her. "Do you want to use another one?"

Jayne didn't attempt to take the card back. "Try entering the numbers. Sometimes the magnetic strip doesn't work."

"I already did that. It's a no-go."

Jayne knew the card was good. Her parents had given it to her two years ago, when they stopped taking her on back-to-school shopping trips and let her go on her own.

She only used it for these trips and gas. Now that she didn't drive, she barely used the thing at all.

Did the company shut down the card?

She turned to Meadow. "Can I borrow your phone?"

The girl handed her the rhinestone-decorated cell. "I told you getting rid of your cell phone wasn't a good idea."

Jayne dialed and waited. "Dad, hey, it's Jayne. I just tried to use the credit card and it didn't work. Did you ever get a letter saying it was canceled or anything?"

The pause on the other end was not a good sign. Finally, her dad said, "Your mom canceled it the other day. I forgot to tell you, and I'm sorry about that."

"She canceled it?" Jayne knew she'd shrieked the question. Meadow, who was in the middle of paying for her own clothes, mouthed "Ow" as she covered one of her ears. "Why did she cancel it?"

"She said something about how you were rude to her at dinner the other night."

Jayne looked down at her feet. She counted to ten. She breathed.

Nothing worked. She was still ready to do battle.

"Kid, I'm sorry about this. I meant to give you my card when you did your back-to-school shopping, but I didn't know you were going today. Will the associate take my card over the phone?"

At that point, Jayne didn't care about the clothes. She didn't care about anything much that had anything to do with her parents and their control issues.

More specifically, Gen and her control issues.

And Dad and his lack of balls when it came to his wife.

"You know what, Dad? I'm sick of this bull crap. Sick. Of. It." She walked out of the store and stood by the railing. She looked down at the first floor with the crowd of people pushing in every which direction. Scurrying the way her parents made her scurry.

For their approval.

For their support.

For friggin' clothes.

"Jayne, I hear you saying that you feel mad. I understand—"

"Dad, spare me. I have Larry for that psychobabble. You want to know something? I'm fine, all things considered. Like, I'm on my way to feeling normal again. But then you and Mom do crap to screw it all up."

She hung up the phone.

Saying those words out loud did a lot more for her than those stupid breathing exercises.

"Hey, you okay, man?" Meadow came to stand beside her, leaning against the railing. "You're not going to have an aneurysm and keel over, are you?"

Jayne laughed. It felt cathartic. Freeing.

Like her old self.

"I'm good. I am, I swear. I just unloaded a bunch of crap just then. And I'm feeling . . . *terrific*." The last word was all but shouted. Half the people below stopped and looked up.

Jayne felt her cheeks get warm.

"So I snagged you something." Meadow walked a few storefronts over until they were out of sight of the boutique they'd just been in. She reached in a bag and pulled out the black shirt with the velvet dragon.

"I can't take that, Meadow. You bought it. It's yours."

Meadow took a mall shopping bag from a stack they were standing by. She put the shirt in it and handed it to Jayne.

"Who said anything about buying it?"

30

YOU SMELL NICE." Darian leaned over and brushed his lips against hers.

"Thanks." Jayne fastened the seat belt and adjusted it so it wasn't cutting her boob in half. Not exactly the look she was going for. "It's my own blend. A little Clinique Happy mixed with some Dove body wash."

Darian kissed the corner of her mouth. "Whatever it is, it makes me want to lick you up." Jayne felt his tongue dart out. "As sweet as I thought."

Jayne wound down the window and the warm night air swept across her face. Thoughts about the credit card and Meadow's five-finger discount were still swirling around in her head.

"You're sure it's okay that I'm coming? Meadow was a little pissed at me today."

Jayne had all but called Meadow a thief. She wouldn't take the bag with the shirt inside, either.

She could pierce her belly button, tattoo her skin, be rude to her mom, tell it like it was to her dad.

But she couldn't steal.

"She likes you plenty. Especially after she sees the gift we're both giving her." He jerked his thumb behind him.

"You should've told me you were getting her something." She fidgeted with the clasp on her bracelet. Darian's bracelet. "I could've helped you look or something. I'm pretty good with girl gifts."

"All's good." He turned onto a street that started to incline sharply. They were on one of the few hills that were in the city known as the Valley. "Mom picked it up for me. She's known Meadow since we started first grade."

Jayne tried to make out what was in the backseat of the sedan, but all she saw was a plastic grocery bag. "What is it?"

"A Louis something or other. It's some kind of big-deal purse girls like."

Meadow was getting a Louis Vuitton? From Darian? Jayne twisted the bracelet around her wrist a few times. She looked down at the bracelet. It looked like he gave all the girls he knew expensive gifts.

"How much do I owe you?" Jayne's stomach twisted. *Stop it, Jayne. Darian's her best friend. Best friends give nice gifts. Tom's given you nice gifts before. Remember that signed Richard Avedon book he got you?*

The memory was little consolation. It made her start thinking about Tom.

"My mom paid for it, so don't worry about it."

His mom picked it out and paid for it. Darian didn't. It was his mom. Jayne felt her heart ache a little less.

"Mom always spends too much money on stuff. Knowing her, she probably spent half of her alimony check on that stupid bag. Wanting people at Nordstrom to think she's still rich, like when her and my dad were still married."

She could tell he was looking at her as they slowly maneuvered up the steep street. Jayne checked. He was.

"If it was me, Meadow would've gotten a birthday card." He grinned at her, his teeth showing white in the inky darkness. "An e-mailed birthday card."

Jayne immediately felt the boulder that had lodged in her throat shift. She looked at the houses that crawled by and started to breathe normally again. "Meadow lives up here? This is pretty nice."

"No, she's out in Gilbert, where it smells like horse crap. Which is really unfortunate, since she lives in the biggest house I've seen in my life." Darian stopped in front of a three-story square house, floodlights shining on the adobe. "This is just a pit stop."

He got out of the car before leaning back in. "I'll be right back, darlin'. The key's still in the ignition if you want to turn on the air conditioner or the radio."

As he made his way up the cement sidewalk, the only sounds Jayne heard were his footsteps and a three-tiered fountain. The air was a tiny bit cooler up here, and Jayne closed her eyes. The running water, the leather seat, and the lingering memory of "darlin'" made her feel like she was living the best moment of her life so far.

About five minutes later, the driver's-side door opened again.

"Got what you needed?" Jayne opened her eyes, a small smile still plastered on her face.

"Hell yeah." Darian was sucking on a cigarette, the orange glow at the end of it getting brighter as he inhaled.

When he exhaled, she realized it wasn't a cigarette.

"I've got some fine, ge-nu-wine skunk here." He held up a brown paper bag.

"Skunk?" The word was barely audible. Somehow, she didn't think he was carrying a carcass in there. The smell kind of told her that.

"Marijuana, darlin'." He started the engine and gently put the bag behind her seat. He took the joint from between his lips and puffed a ring of smoke toward her. "We've gotta bring something to cover up that nasty smell out in farm country."

Jayne jammed her hands between her thighs and the seat. For the life of her, she wanted to look inside that bag. To see if it actually contained what looked like a bag full of pot.

But if the police stopped their car, she didn't want her fingerprints all over it.

Then again, fingerprints would be the least of her worries, what with her probation and all. Just being in a five-foot radius was going to get her in trouble.

Crap. Crap. Crappity crap crap.

The sound of a window going down interrupted her thoughts. Darian flicked his butt outside, and he puffed one more perfect ring in her direction. He looked like a little boy who'd just done something cute.

This was *so* not cute.

"Darian, I don't know if it's such a good idea to have that bag back there what with me on probation and all."

He punched the "1" on the CD changer, and the soft sounds

of some ballad started up. It sounded a lot like what the student body voted on for the theme of last year's homecoming dance.

Jayne didn't know whether she thought Darian's song choice was cheesy or endearing.

"I don't plan on getting pulled over, darlin'." He pulled her hand up on the armrest between them. He clasped it in his larger, stronger, very comforting one. "Just sit back, enjoy the ride, and we'll be at Meadow's in no time."

Jayne tried to relax. She really did. She rolled back her shoulders, stretched her neck to the right, then to the left.

But the tension was there. And so was that bag.

"I can't do this, Darian." They were on the U.S. 60, going a good twenty miles over the speed limit.

She didn't brave a look in Darian's direction. Her head felt cemented in place as she stared at the dark abyss of the floor in front of her.

Jayne kept waiting for him to pull over. And make her walk home.

He lifted her hand and she felt warm, moist lips press against the inside of her wrist. She chanced a look up.

Darian was looking at the road, which was a good thing since they were barreling down the freeway at a good eighty-five, ninety miles an hour. He had a smile on his lips, and he pressed her hand against the smooth, tanned skin of his cheek.

"That bag o' trouble is about to be history." He let go of her hand and pressed the button that released the top of the convertible. It unlatched and started sliding down. Darian reached an arm between the front seats.

He switched to the carpool lane, with its wide shoulder. "Any last words for that troublesome bag of ours?"

She shook her head. She was going to make him a batch of the famous Thompkins chocolate chip cookies. No, make it two.

And maybe even with real sugar.

"Okay then. Off it goes."

Jayne darted a quick look behind them. Nope. No cop cars. At least no marked ones.

"Maybe we should get off the freeway and . . ."

Before she could finish the thought, Darian lifted his arm and let the wind pick up his offering.

Jayne turned to see a thousand-dollar purse fly out of the car.

"Are you crazy?" Jayne screamed over the wind. The car was going close to ninety-five miles per hour, causing currents of air to whip across her cheeks.

"Darlin', what *would've* been crazy was if I'd thrown away that grade-A weed." Darian shot her a look that made her think of the time rotten Aaron Belser had kicked the chair out from under her in Mrs. Tate's first-grade class. "Anyway, Meadow's got a ton of those damn purses that she sells on eBay because she'd rather have the money for her own poison. She'll get loads more fun out of that brown paper sack back there, trust me."

Trust him? Jayne was too busy trying to remember how to breathe and keep her heart from bursting out of her chest like some kind of alien spawn.

But freaking out was the old Jayne. She was now the new and improved Jayne.

The one who was in control of her destiny. The one who had her own mind. And who made her own decisions.

The one who still didn't know what she wanted. Well, who knew that she didn't want drugs in the car. But didn't want to piss off the boy who liked her. What a day.

What a life.

She reached in back and pulled out the bag, using her knuckles and not her fingers. She looked inside.

The bag was almost full of pot. How much did one girl need on her birthday?

"Darian, you got all of this for Meadow?"

"Some of it."

"What's happening with the rest of it?"

Darian took the bag and rolled it back up. He put it back behind Jayne's seat. "Jayne, don't act like you're six."

Jayne twisted the bracelet on her wrist. It felt like a hand-cuff. A shackle tying her to this guy she didn't even know. She remembered her first day at Outreach, when she asked what Darian was doing there.

"I take it you'll be selling this marijuana?"

"Ding, ding, ding, give the girl a prize."

31

JAYNE WENT AHEAD of Darian into the party. If she stayed anywhere near him, she was going to smack him. Or worse.

But she didn't smack him. Instead, she smacked into someone as soon as she entered the dimly lit house. Ellie. And whatever was in her cup sloshed onto Jayne's bare toes.

"Elle?"

"Jaynie." Ellie giggled as she said the word. A tall blond boy stood behind her, his arms around her waist—and touching the underside of Ellie's breasts. "You remember Derek. He's a senior over at East Phoenix High. The one who had that houseboat party, remember?"

Jayne gave him a quick glance. Nothing special there. "I thought you went to the movies with your friends?"

Her sister, slightly unsteady on her feet, said in an overly loud whisper, "As far as Mom and Dad know, I'm at the movies. And I only partially lied. Derek here is a friend."

Ellie wasn't just having problems with her balance. Her words were all slurred. "Friend" had come out in three syllables.

Jayne pulled the drink out of Ellie's hand and sniffed it. She about threw up smelling the stuff. "You could fuel a car on whatever's in here."

Ellie grabbed the drink back, sloshing most of it down the black tank top she was wearing. "You're always such a downer, Jaynie. And just when I thought you'd gotten cool."

Cool? Finding out you're dating a drug dealer, getting belittled by said drug dealer, and getting cheap alcohol spilled onto her all within the last ten minutes had her feeling like the biggest loser in the room.

"Why don't you go home and study or something?" Ellie pointed toward the exit.

Her words plunged straight into Jayne's stomach. First Darian, now Ellie?

Jayne plucked the cigarette out of Ellie's hand. Those breathing exercises were a load of crap. Nicotine, now there was a problem solver.

She took a drag. And felt like she was burning her lungs and the inside of her nose. She dropped it into Ellie's drink.

"Have fun, Elle."

"Hey! Why'd you ruin my drink?"

Jayne put her lips against Ellie's ear. "You're a diabetic, idiot. You will die if you drink too much."

Jayne turned and started toward the front door. Darian was standing there. She turned back around. She felt trapped. She didn't want to stay in here and watch her sister swapping DNA samples. That left the pool, which she saw through the back windows. She headed that way.

And didn't turn back.

• • •

Jayne regretted her decision almost immediately.

Lori and Jenna were smoking on two chaise longues. And Missy Travers, her tennis nemesis, was digging through a cooler and pulling out a bottle of water.

This night just kept getting better and better.

"Jayne? Jayne Thompkins? Is that really you?"

"Missy. Hey."

Missy bounced over, unscrewing the top of the bottle. "You cut your hair. And colored it. And . . . God, you just look so different." She took a swig. "You look like a different person altogether."

Jayne gave her a wan smile and started walking around her. She'd decided about ten seconds ago, when her options out here went from bad to worse, to go back inside, find Ellie, and end the horrible portion of this evening.

"You look really great."

Jayne slowed down. "Yeah?"

"Yeah. Really. I mean, you looked pretty before, but now you're like . . . striking. Gorgeous." She took another drink. "I hope you don't think I'm going all lesbo on you. I just love those makeover shows on TV, and you've had one heck of a make-over."

This was the first time anyone had really said anything nice about her changes. Ellie hadn't liked the change. Tom didn't see why she had to change. Her mom just went postal. Her dad ignored it. Everyone else who liked it hadn't known her for too long.

But Missy, whom Jayne had known since seventh grade, counted as someone who had known her for a long time.

And liked her look.

Missy twisted the lid of her water back and forth, fidgeting. "So, anyway, now that I've got you here, I just wanted you to know I never wanted to be captain." Jayne's face must've showed the disbelief she felt. "Really. I wanted to be more like a cheerleader than a captain, you know? Cheering the girls on during matches, making them signs. Then you broke your arm and I got it."

"You would've gotten it even if I hadn't broken my arm. I was running late the day . . . the day of my accident. And Coach said he'd give you the title if I was late to practice again."

"Whatever. Coach loved you. The girls on the team really loved you."

"I don't think so."

"Jayne, don't be an idiot." What was up with everyone calling her stupid tonight? "You were so focused on winning. You worked on everyone's game to get them to the level they needed to be at to win State. I mean, we did great at State. Third and all, which was awesome. But my doubles game sucked, and a couple of the girls had bad nerves and blew their matches."

Missy fiddled with the bottle. "If you'd been the captain, we would've gotten to first. And maybe I would've made the team at Stanford." She looked up. "I was wondering if maybe you wanted to get together this fall, play some matches with me? Then I could try to get on the team as a walk-on in the spring."

She trailed off, her eyes wide. Expecting an answer.

"I have to say something, Missy. I thought you hated me."

"Hated?" Missy laughed. It sounded a little off, though. "Never hated. Maybe not appreciated. You know, you're not the only one wanting to get into a good school. You have your grades *and* you have tennis. I just have tennis. Colleges love that kind of stuff."

Which was a favorite mantra of Jayne's. So she understood where Missy was coming from. She understood it a lot.

"Yeah, I'll practice with you. But be forewarned. I haven't even picked up a racket since . . . well, April."

Missy swallowed some more water. "By the way, how are you doing?"

Jayne didn't have a chance to answer. "Whatcha doing out here, darlin'?"

Darian was swaggering toward her, a joint in his mouth, a red plastic cup in his hand.

What a nice way to end a perfectly lovely conversation. Having your drug dealer boyfriend interrupt you, drunk.

"Talking."

She turned her back to him. "Missy, you live pretty near me, don't you?"

"I think so."

"Will you give me and Ellie a ride home later?" Jayne avoided looking at Darian.

"Sure thing." Missy's eyes went back and forth between the two of them. "Oh, look at this. I need more water." Missy backed away, full water bottle still in hand. "I'll be back in a minute."

"Hey, you're not mad, are you?" Darian asked.

Jayne ignored the question. She didn't answer stupid questions.

"I'm sorry I got pissy back in the car."

"You were more than just pissy, Darian." Jayne couldn't even look him in the eye. She felt like she'd lost a good friend.

More than a good friend.

"Jayne."

Jerkwad.

"C'mon, Jayne." He'd stepped closer. His breath tickled her cheek. "I was a jerk."

"Yeah, you were." Her arms were still crossed. But Jayne stayed where she was. She was listening. She was still pissed, but she was listening. "And why were you a jerk?"

She wanted to hear him say the words. If he said the right words, maybe she'd give him another chance.

"Because I treated you real bad." He kissed one corner of her mouth.

"And?" At this point, she sort of didn't care if he knew the "and." She liked the kisses. And the words he was saying.

He kissed the other side of her mouth. "And I'm sorry. Sorry for calling you a whatever-year-old." He backed up and looked into her eyes, his hands on both her shoulders. "Sorry for getting too out of it to drive you home."

Jayne felt herself swaying. And she hadn't even had anything to drink.

"Well, well." Jayne smelled the cigarettes before she saw Lori. "Looks like our Jayne here is still with the cute boy. Is the cute boy mentally deficient?"

For a moment, Jayne had a feeling that she was talking to the devil herself.

It was time to send the devil back to hell. "Jealous much, honey?"

32

SOMEBODY KILL me."

"I think you're doing just fine doing that yourself." Jayne stood over the supine figure in Ellie's pink-on-pink-on-pink bedroom. She dropped a bag at the foot of the bed. "The way you chugalugged that stuff last night, you're going to have a nice, early death."

The fully clothed lump groaned.

"Dr. Jayne is here to help you with whatever ails you." She rustled through the bag.

"Can you stop that?" Ellie lowered her voice as if the sound of it was hurting. "I've got a headache."

"Headache, you say?" Jayne reached into the bag and pulled out something round, firm, and red. "Eat this."

A bloodshot eye opened and attempted to focus on her. "What in the hell is that?"

"A persimmon." Jayne carried it to Ellie, who took it tentatively. "The hangover Web sites recommend it for headaches. And so did Dad."

"Dad knows?" Ellie tried to sit up but promptly lay back down again, groaning.

"No. But I remember him saying it once."

"God, be more careful with what you tell me. I about gave myself a coronary." She draped an arm over her eyes. "What time is it?"

"Four-thirty."

"In the afternoon?"

"That's what happens when you go and drink that kind of crap."

Ellie mumbled something.

"What?"

"Everclear."

Jayne didn't know too much about alcohol, but she knew enough to know that was about as close to gasoline as alcohol could get.

"Do you have anything for nausea?" Ellie moaned.

"Ahh." Jayne pulled a bottle out of the bag and handed it over.

"Prickly pear cactus?" Ellie had both bleary eyes on Jayne. "Are you just messing with me?"

Jayne started to the door. "Now, would I do that?"

"Yes."

Jayne smiled. She felt for Ellie and her hangover. She did. She'd had one, and only one. She never planned to have one again.

She was all for learning from her mistakes.

"Where are you going?" Ellie asked.

"Up to my room. I've got a paper for Arizona history due soon."

"Jayne?" The word came out in a throaty whisper.

"Yeah?" Jayne stood there, waiting. Thinking about the 3,200 words she still had to go.

"Did I do anything I'll regret later?"

"Well..."

"Tell me."

"There was some dancing on a table. With some skirt flip-page."

"Holy crap."

Jayne turned to go, ready to get back to the paper. The paper she needed for her A in stupid Arizona history. But she couldn't in good conscience go without being a big sister. She wasn't her sister's keeper anymore, but...

"Elle, you've gotta stop drinking. You're going to find yourself in a really bad position one day—"

"Thanks for the lecture, Jayne." Her tone said she wasn't that thankful. "Don't really feel up to it now, though."

Jayne left. She almost collided with her mom, who was putting on an earring. She was dressed in a pale lavender gown, the bridesmaid uniform picked by the weatherman's fiancée.

"Ellie feeling better with that stomach flu?"

"Why don't you check on her?" Maybe it was time for Ellie to get a dose of Gen, and not just Jayne-buffered Gen.

"Don't have time." Gen checked her makeup in the hallway mirror. "Tell her I'll see her tomorrow. Saturdays are just nuts, with my show this morning and now this wedding. Haven't even said hi to you girls all day."

She air-kissed Jayne, not waiting for an answer. "Have a good night. See what you can do to make up that GPA."

Jayne stood there, left with the smell of Gen's two-hundred-dollar-a-bottle perfume and the feeling she wanted to pierce/cut/tattoo something hanging in the air.

By the time she let herself into Larry's rain forest about an hour later, the anger was full-blown.

She didn't need this Psych 101 crap, but her mom had gone out of her way to drop her off on the way to the wedding.

And Gen had made sure to tell her that, too.

And now she was lying on her back, her forearm covering her eyes, willing herself to feel calmer. Counting to ten.

To twenty.

To 820 by the time Larry came out to get her.

"Are you doing okay, Jayne?"

"Hunky-dory, doc." Jayne eased herself off the couch and walked into his inner office. With each step, she attempted to shake off her mother.

"Can you shut the blinds, please?" The light made her angrier. She closed her eyes, thinking of home. At least there she would've been in her room, blinds shut, comforter over her head.

She heard the plastic slats hit against each other as they closed. "Migraine?" he said.

"Sure." Easier than explaining the real reason.

"You take anything?"

"Don't need to."

Larry didn't say anything, and Jayne concentrated on willing the anger out of her body.

"Jayne?"

"Yeah."

She heard him chuckle softly, non-annoyingly. "If you want, I can get you a magazine. We have a new *National Geographic*, too."

Jayne laughed. Hey, the doc was funny.

"How was your week, by the way?" he asked.

"Long."

"Yeah? Why was that?"

She told him. Pretty much everything. At this point, she didn't care if he told her parents.

A minute or two after she'd finished, he said, "That's quite a week you had."

"What, you don't have those kinds of weeks at your age, doc?" Jayne laughed. She imagined him getting a tattoo and having a friend steal for him and finding out his crush was a drug dealer.

"I'm an old married coot with three kids in college. Those kinds of weeks are few and far between at this point in my life." He chuckled. "Thank God."

A few more minutes passed. The tension seemed to be ebbing out of her. She heard Larry watering, which also helped with the anger thing.

Huh. Maybe this counseling thing really could work.

She picked up the *National Geographic*. It was a new one. She opened it up and started to read while Larry continued to water.

33

"HEY, YOU."

Jayne turned to see Ryan beckoning her over. Like she was a queen and Jayne was her peasant.

Screw that.

Jayne went back to highlighting the Arizona Outreach manual. She'd finally dedicated herself to reading the thing and was about two chapters into it.

"Hey, did you hear me?"

Jayne looked up. Ryan had moved next to her, a manila folder in one hand.

"Maria wants you to help us figure out the schedule for the next couple of weeks."

"Why me?"

Ryan snort-laughed. "Beats me, princess."

"Don't call me that."

"Oh, excuse me, Princess Solitaire."

"I quit playing solitaire weeks ago. And I'm not a princess. I would have one helluva nicer life if I was a princess. So stick to what you know, goth girl."

Jayne pushed herself out of her chair and made her way to Maria's.

That had felt good. Really good. Great, actually.

Maria was on the phone. She was always on the phone. Jayne knocked on the doorjamb.

"Yeah, okay, we'll talk about this later, okay? Thanks." She motioned Jayne in. "Hey, girl. I can't deal with the schedule for August, so could you and Ryan do it for me? Ryan knows the routine, but it's good to brainstorm with someone as you're working on it."

Jayne didn't really want to be in the same room as a person she'd just called "goth girl," much less work with her for a few hours. Stupid bigmouth.

"Sure thing."

Two hours and twenty-eight schedules later, Jayne was ready to call it a day. And maybe rethink her opinion of Ryan.

Maybe she was a goth, but she was smart. She probably did really well on the analytical section of her SAT. The whole "If Person A doesn't like Person C but Person B can only work Tuesdays and . . ." equation was probably a piece of cake for her.

Jayne pretty much just double-checked Ryan's work.

"It's six. You're done for the day about now, aren't you?" Ryan picked up the schedule requests and paper-clipped them together. Ryan was organized, too. An odd concept for someone whose accessories of choice were a dog collar, about twenty piercings (at least to the naked eye), and a blood-red mouth outlined in black liner.

"Sure am." Jayne looked at the clock, looked at the work

they'd just done, and put her head on the table. "I'm tired."

Ryan laughed. "I bet. You really haven't had to do too much critical thinking around this place since you got here."

"Nope." Jayne lifted her head, but rested her chin on her crossed arms.

"Feel like taking a cigarette break with me?"

Jayne smiled. "I don't smoke, but I'll keep you company."

"Only if you don't give me any lectures about cancer."

Jayne solemnly crossed her heart. "I promise there won't be any lectures."

As they walked to the back door of the building, Jayne saw Meadow and Darian had already left their cubicles for the day.

Ryan saw where she was looking. "Yeah, those two are still solitaire king and queen at this place. They always end up leaving fifteen minutes early."

Outside, the door jammed. Jayne leaned against the door and finally got it closed.

"That door likes to stick. One of the many things around here that needs to get fixed one day." Ryan lit a cigarette. "So what's your deal, pr—Jayne. Sorry. Old habits and all."

"What do you mean by 'deal'?" Jayne moved upwind of the cigarette and sat on the curb. The rear of the building had no shade and overlooked the back of a strip mall. Not the prettiest place in the world, but as a cigarette spot, it'd do.

"I mean Meadow and Darian. Why'd you decide to hang out with those two boneheads?"

Jayne shaded her eyes from the sun as she looked up at Ryan. She gave up. The sun was still pretty high and bright. "Meadow's a little boneheadish, I guess, but we're not that close. And Darian . . . I'm still test-driving him."

"Test-driving?" Ryan choked a little on the words as she sat down next to her. "Didn't think I'd hear that coming out of a mouth attached to a person like you."

Jayne rethought the word. Then she realized what Ryan was imagining. "Oh. Oh! No, I don't mean driving as in . . . as in sex." She said the word low and fast. "I mean dating. We're just dating."

They were both silent while Ryan worked on the cigarette. It was a natural, almost relaxing silence.

"Be careful around him, okay?" Ryan stubbed out her cigarette on the curb and got up, putting the butt in the trash next to the door.

"Why is that?"

Ryan shook her head and lit up another cigarette. "I've just heard rumors. I don't want to spread them. But if they're true . . . just watch yourself."

Jayne nodded, absorbing the information. "You know, six out of ten people die of lung cancer in the first year it's detected."

"You promised no lectures, Thompkins." Ryan inhaled long and hard.

"No lecture. Just a factoid. I didn't tell you to quit. *That* would be a lecture."

34

I CAN'T BELIEVE I got stuck in Derby's class." Ellie turned around and started walking backward. Which was brave, considering she was in three-inch platforms walking on one of Palm Desert High's slick floors. Then again, it was only school registration and there was no one to really bump into. "Derby. The guy who always talks to the chalkboard and never to the class."

Jayne started walking faster. So far, she hadn't seen anyone from her grade. She hadn't really expected to, since she'd made Ellie come here at seven.

In the morning.

Then again, Ellie had managed to put on heels and makeup. And had drunk a Red Bull on the way over.

"Jayne."

So much for having any luck. The distance to the door looked about five yards away.

She'd ignored Miss Challen last semester, at the Fourth of July party, even earlier today when the adviser had stopped her blue Volvo to let Jayne and Ellie cross the street.

The time had come, though. That inevitable conversation. It was either going to happen now, a week from now, or a month from now.

It might as well be now. She turned, a fake Gen smile in place.

"Hey, Miss Challen."

The adviser wore white sweatpants and a "I'd Rather Be Kayaking" shirt with a coffee stain splattered on her left boob. "I'm glad I was a klutz with my coffee. If I wasn't forced to get up from my desk, I might've missed you."

If only, Jayne thought to herself.

"Have you registered for classes yet?"

Jayne nodded and looked over the woman's shoulder. She so didn't want to be here making small talk with Miss Challen. Especially small talk about classes.

Because she was going to be lying through her teeth.

"I heard honors calculus is going to give everyone a great foundation for college math. Be it at Arizona State or Harvard"—she gave Jayne a wink—"for a girl like you, Jayne."

"Sounds good." Jayne shuffled her feet and kept avoiding the redhead's eyes. Today Miss Challen wore her hair in a low ponytail, with flyaway tendrils sprouting out around her head.

"You're on track with all your honors work, right, Jayne?" She waved a hand in front of her. "Last quarter was just a glitch. Your GPA is still healthy and Harvard-ready."

Jayne looked at Miss Challen, searching for the lie. "Really?"

"Really." Miss Challen leaned closer. "Do you want me to tell you what your standing is?"

Knowing Miss Challen and her respect for people's privacy,

she probably wanted to make sure Jayne was okay with Ellie overhearing her.

"Yes." She braced herself. "What's my number?"

Miss Challen leaned closer. "Six."

Six? "Do you mean sixty?"

"No, number six. You're in the top one percent, Jayne. Which is a great place to be."

She was that high up, after that many B's and C's?

Jayne wondered briefly what kinds of grades everyone else got at Palm Desert. And how much worse she could do and still get in the top five percent of the class.

She snapped out of her calculations when she realized the counselor was still talking to her. "Now, are you all set with your classes? Is there anything I can help you with?"

"I'm on track. No worries here." Jayne hooked her arm through Ellie's. "I have to get Ellie home. I'll talk to you later."

And with that, she guided her sister through the double doors and into the 120-degree weather outside. Out here, Jayne felt she could breathe again.

"Why'd you lie to Challen? Especially when you found out your GPA?" Ellie was tiptoeing through the gravel parking lot in her three-inch platforms. Jayne dropped her arm from around Ellie's.

"I didn't lie. I just didn't tell her I was on the non-honors track."

"Are you going to change your schedule, now that you know your GPA?"

Jayne shrugged. "We'll see."

She was excited about her GPA. But she was also excited

about having a life with a boyfriend and having a schedule that wouldn't compete with that.

Jayne looked over at the spot where she used to park the Jetta. A four-door sedan from the eighties was parked there. Someone had written CLEAN ME in the dust on its back window. They passed the car as they headed toward the bus stop another block away.

In the distance, Jayne made out a familiar brown head. She was about to call out to Tom when she saw him laughing.

And who he was laughing with.

Lori.

35

Jayne PUT a Leash on Britney and put the dog's collapsible water bowl in her bag. She also collected a couple of plastic bags for Britney's poop.

They were going to go for a very, very long walk. So long a walk, Britney would probably have to be carried home.

But Jayne didn't mind carrying her. She had so much rage over the whole Lori/Tom thing, she could've walked to Washington and back. (Okay, maybe Washington Street and back. But that was still a good fifteen miles away.)

She had her baseball cap, sunscreen, and two liters of water. She was ready.

"Hey, hon. You want company?" Her dad walked from behind his desk, a jaunt in his step. "I was trying to solve a problem with that skin-care line and I just really need a break. Do you mind?"

Did she mind? Well, Britney didn't. She was already pawing at the door, trying to get out, her little tongue hanging to the side and dripping on the floor.

Jayne didn't know how to turn him down without hurting his feelings. She shook her head. "No, I'd love the company."

"Great. Give me a minute to put on my shoes."

As she watched him go upstairs, she thought, *We'll walk and do small talk. It's not like I'm going to talk to him about anything big, anyway.*

"And the blog had me in an electric chair, my head . . . smoking, I guess."

It had been two hours and about two miles of walking. After the first mile of Jayne talking about Brenda Deavers having been Jenna Deavers's sister, Lori flirting with Tom, and Meadow trying to get her to shoplift, her dad made her stop at the first outdoor café with a misting system outside.

Britney had a bowl of water and shade. Her dad had a glass of wine and a lot of questions.

Jayne was glad she didn't bring up Ellie's drinking or Darian being a pot dealer. Her dad seemed to have enough information to deal with.

"And this is on a blog. One of those online things everyone can see?"

She nodded. Shrugged. What else was there to do?

Her dad wiped a hand over his face. "Jayne, Jayne, Jayne. What has been going on in this life of yours? I feel like I'm totally out of the loop."

Jayne fiddled with the straw in her glass of Diet Pepsi. "It's not like I'm twelve anymore, you know? Where you have to fix my problems because I'm not smart enough to figure them out."

"Jaynie." Her dad leaned over and put a hand on hers. "Do you really think handling problems is about being able to fix them yourself? At, what, sixteen years old? I'm forty-five and I'm always turning to people to help me out."

"Yeah?" She'd never thought about that. Then again, she'd never seen her dad ask for help.

"Yeah. Like the dean of the department down at U of A, or the chemist at the lab, or your mom."

"Mom?" Now she knew he was lying.

"Your mom's always been a great problem solver. An amazing problem solver. That was one of the things that attracted me to her."

Jayne pulled her hand away and sat back. "But didn't her walking all over you and everyone else in her life turn you off?"

There. She said what she'd been thinking since she was thirteen and started noticing things.

Her mom never hugging her dad when he got home.

Her mom never asking how his day was.

"How do I put this." He wiped his brow with the moist napkin under his glass. "I'm the sensitive one in this relationship. I make sure you girls have your birthday presents and the I love you's. But your mom is missing, as someone I don't remember once said, that sensitivity chip. So she doesn't do that."

"How do you put up with her treating you like . . . like dirt?"

"For example . . . ?"

"For example, when she comes home and doesn't hug you. Or ask how your day was."

"She doesn't hug because she's not so good at displays of affection. And the 'how's the day going' thing . . . she calls me at work and we discuss it then. Never at home. We don't want to bring our work home." In a lower voice, he added, "She's especially tense nowadays because she's getting older. And older is not good in her industry."

"So is her childhood responsible for all her crap?" Jayne rolled her eyes. She couldn't help it.

"No. Her adulthood. You've probably figured out that she's still regretting ending up at a state school over an Ivy League."

"Which I don't get. She's a journalist. ASU has a good journalism department."

"You know that. I know that. All your mother sees is how her best friend from high school got into an Ivy League and is now at CNN."

This was news to Jayne. She'd never heard that, ever. "Who?"

Her dad said the name, and Jayne knew the name. Almost everyone did. She was big. Huge.

And looked almost exactly like her mother.

36

JAYNE. LEE. THOMPKINS. What is that on your back?" Gen was livid.

At the end of their walk, Jayne had told her dad about the belly-button piercing and the tattoo. He told her that he couldn't keep those two things from her mother. "A lot of the things you told me today can be kept between us, Jayne. Your mom knowing one way or another won't matter. But you putting a hole and permanent ink onto the body that she gave birth to ... she needs to know."

Now she knew.

"Well, you'll be getting that lasered off next week. End of discussion."

They were back home, and everyone was in the study. Jayne, Gen, Dad. The only one missing was Ellie.

She was at the mall with her credit card. A working credit card. A reward for never having yelled at Gen.

"And don't think it's going to be that easy, young lady. Your allowance is going to pay for this little adventure of yours. As it is, you'll never see a red cent from us ever again." Her mom seemed to be building steam.

Jayne didn't say anything. She was staring at one of her mom's local Emmys. She wondered if she walked over to the shelf, grabbed that Emmy, and smashed it on the floor, if that would be the last straw.

Would Gen disown her? Or would she be threatened with yet another weekly visit with Larry?

"What exactly is on your back, anyway?" Jayne's dad asked.

"Who the hell cares, Sean? Does it matter?"

"It does to Jayne." He gestured for her to come to him. "C'mon, let's take a look."

Jayne went over and pulled her shirt high enough so he could see the line of words curlicued over the waistband of her mid-rise jeans.

"'What does not destroy us—we destroy, and it makes us stronger.'"

"Really, Jayne, couldn't you have at least picked something less morbid?" Her mom stirred a straw through her iced tea. "Like a heart or a daisy?"

"I didn't feel like a heart or a daisy or a bunny rabbit, Mother." Jayne fell back onto the sofa, her eyes closing, shutting the sight of Gen out. "I felt like getting this put on as soon as I saw it on the wall at the tattoo parlor."

Crystal hit wood. Her mom was definitely ticked. She hadn't even attempted to place the glass on the coaster a couple of inches away. "You didn't even plan to put those words on you?

And what, did the tattoo artist pick where to put it so he could look at your ass all day?"

Jayne didn't waste the breath to correct her. Mabel had seemed like she didn't care one way or another what her ass had looked like.

"How about this?" Her dad put his hands up. "If Jayne can answer one question, she can keep that tattoo. At least for a month while we get used to it," he added when his wife started to sputter.

"I don't know what you've been smoking, Sean." Gen pushed the palms of her hands into her closed eyelids. "Her body is ours until she's eighteen. Hell, everything she has, between that room of hers, that car she can't drive anymore, even the smarts that got her A's most of her life—it's all ours."

Jayne could only stare at her mom. Was that what she really thought? That everything she was and had belonged to Gen and Sean Thompkins?

"Gen, you're toeing the line." Her dad seemed to be giving his wife a look of warning. "Stay on the right side of it."

Her mom looked like she wanted to say more vile stuff, but she pursed her lips and took another sip of iced tea. Which was a good thing, considering the thoughts Jayne was still having about those Emmys of hers.

"What was your question, Dad?"

He steepled his fingers together. He arched his eyebrows, and his eyes sparkled. "If you get this answer right, we'll give this whole tattoo business a rest. At least until next month, when we'll revisit how we're all feeling about the matter."

Jayne nodded. "Agreed."

"Okay then." His eyes seemed to grow even more amused. "Who was the person who first said that quote on your back? And"—he held up a finger—"from which of his works did it come from?"

It looked like someone had come home after their walk and had been on the Internet.

"Who is Friedrich Nietzsche, in *Maxims of a Hyperborean*."

Her dad laughed. "That is correct."

Her mom dropped her head back on the sofa, looking at the ceiling. "Mother—."

37

Darian's hand was on her boob. It was on her boob, and the only things separating his skin from hers were her bra and the black cotton of her shirt.

"God, you feel great, Jayne." His nose was buried in her neck, his tongue tracing a trail around her ear.

"You feel pretty good yourself." They were sitting on a couch outside Meadow's house. It was Friday, the last Friday before school started up again.

It was cause for celebration. It was cause for Jayne to let Darian feel her boob.

Oh my lord. A boy's hand is on my breast.

In her head, Jayne shrieked a little. Partly out of excitement for where Darian's hand was. Partly out of terror for where Darian's hand was.

They'd been kissing out here for a good twenty, thirty minutes. And for the first time, Jayne hoped her sister couldn't see her. Ellie had come to the party with them. Mainly because Jayne didn't want to be caught by surprise running into Ellie drunk and belligerent again.

"Jayne?"

"Yeah?" This was terrific. She wondered why she'd been riding Ellie so hard about this whole kissing deal. It felt pretty friggin' amazing.

"Let's go upstairs."

"Why?" She said this after another long, intense kiss.

"Why?" He pulled back. Laughed. "I'll give you one guess. If you win, we go upstairs; if you lose, we go upstairs."

It felt like someone had poured a bucket of cold water over her head. She pushed back. The hand on her breast felt clumsy and uncomfortable. She pulled it off her.

As she sat there, her senses heightened. She heard the couples around her whispering and kissing. She smelled the smoke coming from the corner where a bunch of girls sat and talked and laughed.

"C'mon . . ." He tried to kiss her. She pushed him away.

Darian shot off the couch, his hands combing through his hair. "I knew it. Meadow told me, but I wouldn't believe her. Criminy!"

"Knew what?" But Jayne knew the answer.

"That you were a tease. That you only were good for kissing and groping. Crap!"

Jayne felt the girls in the corner watching them. "Darian. C'mon." She tried to sound light and teasing. Part of her didn't know why she wasn't yelling or cursing. "This isn't really that big a deal, is it?"

He looked at her, his hands on his knees, his head about a foot from hers. "The only way this isn't going to be a big deal is if there's some small . . . token of affection I get tonight."

"Token?" That word did nothing to make her feel better.

"A token. Where there's no risk of disease or pregnancy. But I get what I want, and all's good."

It took a minute to work out the word puzzle, but when she did she started laughing. She couldn't help it. The laughter just kept bubbling up inside of her. "Let me get this straight. You get yours. I get nothing—"

"You got something—an eight-hundred-dollar bracelet."

"You said that came with no strings."

"Everything has strings, Jayne, everything!" He all but whined this last part.

"I guess I can't handle the strings, then."

After she said the words, she realized that she didn't feel one iota of sadness. *A token.* Whatever. A token got you on the bus.

Jayne leaned her head back and looked at the clear, starry sky. *A token. Ha!* The words kept replaying as she worked on the clasp at her wrist. When she unfastened it, she held the rope of gems out to him.

He stared at the bracelet and then gave her his puppy-dog eyes. His voice got softer, lower. Whiny. "Couldn't you suck me off just once?"

Jayne stared at the boy in front of her. She felt like she wasn't even in her body anymore.

She got up and pushed the bracelet into his chest until he was forced to reach up and take it. "I have to get going. Have a good life, Darian."

She turned and left him still staring at her with those puppy-dog eyes. She shivered. Crazy how she'd been into him one second, letting him go with his hand where no one had gone before. And now?

Now he gave her the heebie-jeebies.

She walked by the table of girls, the tips of their cigarettes the only things she could make out in the dark corner. "You break up, Jayne?"

She peered deeper into the shadows. The question sounded like it came from Meadow. "Yep."

"Before or after he asked you for his token?"

"After."

She heard Meadow laugh. Joylessly. Knowingly. "Darian's not too good about going a night without sex. Guess you found that out."

Jayne had her hand on the sliding glass door. It was late and she was more than ready to forget about Darian and the out-of-body conversation she was having right now.

But she couldn't help herself. Meadow wasn't making any sense.

"We've been going out a couple of months now," Jayne said. "He seemed okay with not having sex."

There was that laugh again. "Sweetie, do you really think he left you after each date to go back home? He's a senior, he's on the basketball team, and he's cute." The tip of her cigarette grew brighter as she took another drag from it. "He was off screwing anything that moved when he wasn't with you."

38

Jayne just wanted to go home and forget about this night. And these people.

"Has anyone seen my sister?"

The consensus was that she was upstairs in the master bedroom. Passed out.

Jayne ran. Faster than she ever had in her life.

A naked, still form was in the center of the bed.

"Ellie, wake up. Wake up!" She shook her, but that did nothing.

Jayne searched frantically in the dark for clothing. Where the hell was her underwear? And her dress?

She found them tossed on the back of the desk chair. She started pulling Ellie's legs through the holes of her underwear.

"Is everything okay?"

Jayne turned to quickly glance over her shoulder. Meadow was there. She seemed . . . well, not indifferent, which was something for Meadow. "No. Help me put this dress over her head."

Together they lifted Ellie's torso off the bed, slipped the hem of the dress down, and slid it the rest of the way to her knees.

After Ellie was fully dressed, Jayne put her face in front of Ellie's. "Ellie!"

Her sister's eyes were closed, but she was moaning.

"Ellie!"

She shook her sister's shoulders. Nothing. "Meadow, did you see if my sister was drinking anything?"

"I think she had a drink, but it wasn't like she was throwing them back or anything." Meadow zipped up Ellie's dress. "Jayne, you should know that Lori took a picture of Ellie with her cell phone."

Jayne was shocked into stillness. "What? Why?"

Meadow shrugged. "She's a freak."

Jayne went back to the chair and found Ellie's purse. *Please, Ellie, for once, please have been responsible.* She opened the clasp.

Inside was Ellie's glucose meter.

Jayne went to Ellie and punched the meter into the tip of Ellie's finger. Normal was around 170 mg/dl at this time of night.

Right now, Ellie's blood sugar was at 400.

"Go and get me some water. Now."

Meadow left while Jayne reached for Ellie's cell phone and dialed the pre-programmed number. While she waited for someone to pick up, she put pillows under Ellie's feet to help keep the blood flowing to her head.

"Nine-one-one. What is your emergency?"

"My sister. She's in diabetic shock."

"Jayne!"

Jayne looked up from the tile she'd been staring at. She'd

been wondering what had made the scuff marks, and what kind of solvents it would take to clean them up.

She'd been like this for the last twenty minutes or so. Ever since she had ridden in the ambulance with Ellie to Camelback Regional.

The same hospital Jayne had been brought to just four months ago.

Her mom was running down the corridor, and the only thought in Jayne's mind was that it would really suck if her mom's heels slipped out from under her.

Then all three Thompkins women could be admitted to this hospital.

Random thought. Then again, this was a random kind of night.

"Jayne, I asked you a question. How'd this happen?"

Jayne had been asking the same thing herself. Ellie had been eating like crap all summer. And she didn't think her sister had been good about being consistent with her shots.

Then again, getting a shot three times a day, every day, year after year, could get to a person.

But Jayne didn't really know the answer. She could only guess. So she settled with what she knew: "I don't know."

"You don't know?" Gen's face was getting red. She must've been getting ready for bed when Jayne had called from the ambulance. Her face was free of makeup, her hair was in a ponytail. That of course meant she was wearing a baseball cap and sunglasses. Jayne checked her watch.

1:32 A.M.

"No. I don't know what Ellie put into her body or didn't. At first I thought she was drunk, but then I checked her blood glucose levels. That's when I figured out she was in shock."

"Gen!" Jayne's dad walked toward them, fast and determined. He'd gone to see the doctor as soon as her parents had gotten there. "The doctor wants to see us." He started toward the next set of double doors.

"You stand right here, young lady. Don't even think about moving a muscle."

Jayne's night had been filled with threats, disclosures, and child pornography. She wasn't about to take her mom's crap and see what kind of punishment she'd get because her mom was dealing with misplaced mother-guilt issues. (Her sessions with Larry were pretty quiet, but she picked up a few of his psychology journals when he didn't have a new *National Geographic*.)

"Or what?"

"Or what?" Gen said the words like she couldn't believe Jayne had even dared to speak them. "Or what? Fine, let's get down to brass tacks. You will be going to a boot camp. Or you will be going on my show to talk about this downward spiral you've been having. Or—"

Her mom stopped, taking in a sharp breath. She wanted to say something else. Jayne could see it. She could *feel* it.

"Or what, Gen?"

The use of her first name pushed her mother over the tiny edge she'd been holding on to. "Or else you will leave my house."

"Good to know where we stand, Gen." Jayne felt a calm she'd never felt in her life. It made her think more clearly. And made the irrational thoughts she was having seem almost rational.

"You may also want to know that while Ellie was in the middle of what everyone mistook for being plastered, Lori—Diane's stepdaughter—took off Ellie's clothes and captured it with her camera phone."

Well, it looked like Gen was speechless. Good. It made Jayne almost want to tell her more. About how when she first saw Ellie, she thought she'd been drugged and raped. Meadow had told her later that Lori had been blabbing all night about what she planned to do with Ellie. To get back at the Thompkinses.

Speechless, Gen turned and followed the path her husband had already taken. She'd pulled her phone out and had it open. To call the police? To call Diane?

Jayne didn't know. And she didn't care.

The house was quiet. And dark. Jayne didn't even close the front door. She was only going to be here a minute.

She went upstairs and looked for Piggy. She found him where she'd last hidden him: in the air duct over her closet.

She'd had Piggy since she was born. Tooth-fairy money had gone in there. Birthday money. Christmas money.

Piggy was the size of a piglet. There had to be a good stash in there. Jayne shifted the ceramic pink pig from hand to hand. It felt like a big stash.

She looked at the wall her mom had had the decorator paint white when Jayne wanted red.

She drew her hand back. The hand holding Piggy.

She threw him at the blank wall, where he shattered in all directions.

Where his guts exploded in all directions. Green, paper guts.

· · ·

The bus was empty. Jayne had known it would be, but not *empty* empty.

Jayne hugged her backpack closer to her. She sat in the very back, in the corner, her head supported by two sides of bus.

A tiny sound had her opening her zipper a little more. "You okay, Brit?"

A wet black nose and tiny tongue licking her hand answered in reply.

"I don't know where we're going yet, but you're up for the adventure, right?" Another lick answered her.

She'd been all set to leave—money, a week's worth of underwear, the camera she'd gotten at Christmas and had been too insanely busy or numb to use—when Britney had all about tripped her as she started out the door. Those big ebony eyes of hers had looked at Jayne with such hope. Such love.

Jayne had gotten the leash, a collapsible water dish, and a box of dog treats. When the bus had come, she'd put the very happy stowaway in her backpack.

And now they were traveling companions on Bus 84 at four-thirty on a Saturday morning. Her sister was in intensive care, her mom never wanted to see her again, her boyfriend was an ass, and her best friend . . . he didn't seem like he wanted to be her best friend anymore.

Jayne hugged her backpack and dog closer to her. She didn't have anywhere to go.

She didn't have anyone to go to.

39

SIX-THIRTY A.M. on a Saturday is calm, peaceful, quiet.

It's also the worst time of day for a teenage girl who just desperately wants to sleep.

Jayne was one such girl. She hadn't let herself go to sleep on the bus. That was a great way to be a target. And after the past twenty-four hours, she definitely was not going to be a target for yet another person.

The adrenaline had left her, and exhaustion had started to seep through her bones. And right when she wanted to cry because she was so tired, she remembered something.

There was a cot in Maria's office at Outreach Arizona. The place was closed because Maria had to go to some conference today in North Phoenix. And if that glitchy door in back hadn't latched properly . . . she could get in.

She knew it was a long shot that it wasn't latched now. But a long shot was better than the nothing she currently had.

She held her breath when she was standing in front of that door fifteen minutes later. She closed her eyes and swallowed. She felt Britney sit on her foot.

Her eyes still closed, she whispered, "Feeling lucky, Brit?"

Her thumb pressed down, and her arm pulled at the heavy door.

It opened. Britney started barking. That might've been because Jayne was jumping up and down and singing, "The door is open, yes it's true, the door is open, let's use the loo!"

"Princess?"

Jayne turned the other way on the stiff cot. When was she going to stop dreaming about the Outreach program? It was like there was something in the air that made her keep having weird dreams. Like the one she'd just had about Darian stalking her around the cubicles, his penis hanging out.

"Hey, Jayne. This isn't a Motel 6."

Jayne cracked open her eyes, hoping that this was just another one of her dreams where Ryan was a ringmaster, whip in hand, and Jayne was trying to figure out how to do a handstand on an elephant.

Nope. This was real-life Ryan. No whip. Just a chain around her neck.

"What're you doing here?" Jayne's voice came out hoarse. She looked at her watch. It was two o'clock. It was the middle of a Saturday, the last Saturday before school, and she was hiding out in the Outreach center, nothing but dog biscuits, a snoring dog, and a week of underwear as her possessions.

"I left something in my desk."

"You have a key?" Jayne had heard that Maria was the only one with a key. Something about not trusting any of the delinquents around here enough to have a copy.

"Yeah, I have a key." Ryan seemed offended, based on her tone and scowl. "But you don't. How'd you get in?"

"The sticky door by the Dumpster. Where we sat outside and you smoked the other day."

Ryan rolled her eyes. "I *told* Maria she needed to do more than just WD-40 it."

Jayne sat up, and she felt dizzy. She put her head in her hands. "Well, I for one am glad it didn't work."

She looked up when Ryan didn't say anything. The girl was staring at her bemusedly, a finger hooked over her chain. "You hungover or something?"

Jayne laughed. "No. I'm the furthest thing away from a hangover right now."

"Then why do you look like you are?" Ryan had a note of disbelief in her voice.

Jayne stood up, and the motion made her even dizzier. But she kept on her feet. Her pride wouldn't let her sink back down to the cot. "Maybe because I have just had the worst night of my life."

Britney leaned against her leg, and Jayne picked her up, thankful for having at least one buddy on her side. She buried her nose against Britney's dog-scented neck.

Jayne looked up when the silence seemed to be stretching for an eternity. Ryan was looking at her fingernails, picking at the black polish.

Without looking up, she asked, "You hungry?"

"Yeah. I am."

"What's your dog's name?"

"Britney. Britney Spears Federline."

Ryan looked up. Was there a tiny little smile on her mouth? Nah, Jayne was imagining it. She was so starved for company, she actually thought Miss Unsocial here was warming up to her.

"Well then, Jayne. You can bring your bitch with us if you want." She started toward the door. Jayne followed.

"But Jayne?"

"Yes, Ryan?"

This first-name business was weird. Oddly satisfying, but weird.

"If she piddles on my upholstery, I'm going to turn Britney into a rag. Okey-dokey?"

40

FEEL LIKE GETTING some breakfast?" Ryan had come out of nowhere, and was now jingling her car keys.

Jayne looked up from the computer she was at. It was 6 A.M. on Sunday and she was trying to look for an apartment with the $887 Piggy had given his life for.

So far, nothing. Not with security deposits. Pet deposits. First and last months' rent.

It looked like it was time to find someone needing a roommate. And who lived in a cheap part of town that wouldn't scare the bejeezus out of her.

"Or have you had something already?" Ryan squatted next to Jayne and rubbed behind Britney's ears. The two had bonded over bacon scraps and an afternoon walk the day before.

"Nope." She clicked off the computer. Apartment searching could wait. "And you're just in time, too. Those dog biscuits were looking mighty tempting."

• • •

"Okay, stalker, how'd you know about this place?"

"What?" Ryan pulled her Jeep into a space and turned off the engine.

"It's just this place. It's my favorite place in the world." They were parked outside All the Sweet Tomorrows. Her and Ellie's place. And most of Paradise Valley's place, judging by the line winding its way around the building.

"I know."

"See? You're my stalker."

Ryan got out and slammed the door. Jayne followed suit. "I heard you going on and on about it to Meadow one day."

"Ryan, I didn't know you cared." Jayne batted her eyelids.

The other girl laughed as she adjusted one of the black leather cuffs that encircled her forearm. "Yeah, well, a person doesn't forget a name like All the Sweet Tomorrows. Sounds like a stupid romance novel."

"I know. Isn't it great?"

Two blueberry muffins and two macchiatos later, Jayne saw a familiar face making her way through the parking lot.

"Oh my lord. Maria's here. What a small . . ." Jayne trailed off as she realized Ryan wasn't looking toward Maria or at her. "Hey, you rat." Ryan looked up. "Did you have Maria meet us here?"

Ryan shrugged. Before Jayne could ask anything else, Maria was at their table.

"Ladies! Fancy meeting you! Let me grab something and I'll be right back."

The way the woman had just plopped her purse down and

hadn't even asked to join them, Jayne was a hundred percent certain that Ryan had set her up.

A tiny part of her was relieved. Now that it was day two of Jayne Finding Her Independence, she was so over it.

She was tired. And wanted a real bed.

But she still didn't want to go home.

"And so then you got on the bus, came to the Outreach center, and have been living there ever since?" Maria took another sip of herbal tea, her scone long since gone.

"In a nutshell."

"God, Jayne, how scary."

Jayne felt her lip quiver and she forced a smile. Yeah, it had been scary. Mainly because she didn't know what she was going to do about food, shelter, and all the stuff a person needs to survive.

And $887 wasn't going to help her survive for long.

She concentrated on pressing her finger against the errant crumbs from her muffin. As she rubbed them off onto her napkin, her eye landed on a person at the register.

Mrs. Deavers.

Jayne felt like she'd grown roots. She couldn't have moved—or rather, hidden—if she'd wanted to. She watched as the woman paid for a pink box of some kind of pastry. She heard the woman behind the counter say, "And we used the yellow frosting, just as you asked, to spell out 'Happy Birthday Jenna.'"

Mrs. Deavers nodded and said something inaudible. Jayne noticed, for the first time, a little girl clinging to her leg.

A little girl with the same amber hair and big brown eyes her sister had had.

Jayne found she was straining to hear what Mrs. Deavers was saying. Like, "That girl over there is the one who killed your sister. Hate her. Everyone should hate her."

Immediately, Jayne felt like the selfish, self-centered person she knew she was being. *Yes, Jayne, that's right. Worry about how Mrs. Deavers is going to point you out. Like that's her number-one priority right now.*

And as she sat there arguing with her conscience, Mrs. Deavers turned. And stared at Jayne. At first she stared through her. The hair did that to people nowadays.

But then Mrs. Deavers recognized her. Jayne could tell by the way she kept staring. And then the eventual recognition dawning in her eyes.

There was deep, deep sadness there. She looked for the anger, but couldn't find any.

At this moment, Jayne would've preferred the anger. It didn't hurt as much as looking at someone else's grief.

"C'mon, honey, let's go." Mrs. Deavers's hands were shaking as she paid her bill.

Mrs. Deavers didn't look at her again. In fact, she seemed to be doing everything in her power to keep from looking in Jayne's direction.

"Can I get a cupcake?" the little girl asked.

"Not today, honey. Let's get going, okay?"

A few seconds later, they were gone.

"Jayne, was that the mother?"

Jayne turned to see Maria looking at her, her cup of coffee in her hands, her own eyes concerned. Maria didn't say the rest. "Jayne, was that the mother of the little girl you hit?" But she didn't have to.

Jayne closed her eyes and nodded. There were too many people in here to start crying.

After a couple of minutes of the crowd talking, laughing, and clinking coffee cups, Maria spoke again. "You know, there's something to be said about the twelve steps."

"Are you talking AA?" Jayne didn't know where Maria was going with this.

"No, just the steps. The one I'm thinking of right now, based on your reaction to Mrs. Deavers, is step nine. Making amends."

Jayne was looking outside. Watching as the Deaverses' car—the same red sedan, with all the dents banged out and painted over—pulled away.

Minus one less child.

"I have a feeling you're wanting to make amends. Am I correct in assuming this?"

Jayne nodded. The car disappeared from view.

"The ninth step also says not to make amends if it might hurt the other person more than it helps them."

Jayne met Maria's eyes. "You know, just now, when I saw Mrs. Deavers there, I wanted to apologize. But for the longest time, I've wanted to send her a letter, telling her she was more to blame than I was." She looked at the packets of sugar on the table. "But I never sent the letter. There was always something holding me back."

Maria nodded. There was nothing in her eyes that looked like she was thinking any less of Jayne. "That's one of those steps of grief. Denial. You got over it, though. You've moved on." She touched Jayne's arm. "You're not a bad person, Jayne. You're human, dealing with some pretty hard-core human emotions."

Jayne felt the tears coming. Stupid Maria with her kind smile. "Being human sucks sometimes."

Maria smiled, and covered one of Jayne's hands with hers. "I couldn't agree with you more, m'dear."

41

"THanks For coming WITH me."

"No problem. If you hadn't asked, I was going to offer." Maria turned onto the quiet street that held multimillion-dollar homes.

Ryan leaned forward from the backseat, her head swiveling right and left as she took in the houses. "Are you sure I can't call you princess?"

Jayne heard the teasing tone and didn't take offense. "I think I've earned my non-princess stripes these last couple of days, don't you think?"

"Yep. Although I have to say, you got your initiation when Darian got all rapist frat boy on you."

Jayne had told Ryan pretty much everything that'd been happening in her life between the day of the accident and the night she ran away. In comparison, Ryan's life seemed downright uneventful. A high school coach for a mom and a CPA for a dad.

So much for having a life that matched the piercings, tattoos, and attitude. Ryan had explained them away by saying, "Middle-class boredom, plain and simple."

Jayne's wandering thoughts brought her back to what had made them start to wander—Darian. And what she now knew about him.

"Maria?"

"Yeah?"

"Did you tell Darian why I was at the Outreach program?"

"Nope. Too busy for that kind of small talk." Maria pulled into the wide half-circle driveway, stopping at the three-tiered fountain.

"That's what I thought."

"Why?" she asked.

"He told me once he knew why I was there. And that he found out because you'd told him."

"No, didn't say a word. He must've recognized you from when you were in the newspapers."

"I couldn't believe you hooked up with that pond scum, any-way." Ryan carried Britney as they walked to the door.

"Well, I didn't know he was pond scum at the time." They were only a few steps from the front door. Was it too late to run? "It would've been nice if you had told me."

Ryan concentrated on adjusting Britney's collar. "You know, you weren't the only one in the news." She looked up. "He was in there for stealing."

"Stealing?" She thought back to the Louis Vuitton bag, the bracelet. "He's not rich?"

Ryan laughed. "His mom works the night shift at Denny's."

"But he has a BMW."

"He installs replacement glass at the dealership. He must borrow cars."

Jayne thought about the time she asked Ryan if he was a drug dealer. "You said it was drugs."

"I was guessing."

Jayne lowered her voice so only Ryan heard. "He sort of is a drug dealer."

"Get out!"

Before Jayne could say anything else, the door jerked open. The uncertainty she'd been feeling all weekend heightened, and she felt like she was going to puke.

Jayne's mom stood there, her dad's arm around her. She looked like hell. No makeup. No hat. No sunglasses.

Before Jayne could say anything, 120 pounds of mom came flying at her. "Jayne. Thank God. Thank God."

Jayne's nerves and loneliness started to ease from her shoulders. Not completely, though. There was no chance.

Her mom was hugging her too hard. "I'll give you back the credit card. I should've never canceled it. And I'm sorry about everything. For not understanding how the accident was affecting you, for saying I didn't want you in the house."

Jayne felt a warm hand on her cheek. She looked up to see her dad, tears in his eyes.

She knew the words Gen was saying had come from her dad. Her mom wasn't this intuitive.

"She's been worried that you were out on the streets, no money, selling your body to make ends meet."

Okay, so *that* sounded like her mom.

Gen sniffed and hugged her harder. "I did a story on a girl who did that once. I never want to have to worry about that with you."

Jayne opened her mouth to defend herself. Her honor. Her ethical code. Then she saw her dad shaking his head. He mouthed, *She is who she is.*

Out loud, he said, "Welcome home, kiddo."

42

YOU'RE SUCH A NUMBNUT." Jayne felt tears pricking her eyes, seeing Ellie lying there in the white sheets of the hospital bed. Covered with IVs.

"Nice to see you too, nerd."

Jayne sat gingerly on the side of the bed and reached for one of Ellie's hands.

"I really fouled it up this time, huh?" Ellie attempted to smile. The attempt was lopsided, but at least the attempt was made.

"Based on the picture I saw, yeah."

"Picture?" Ellie's whisper got slightly louder.

"It's been taken care of. No worries." The phrase reminded her of Darian. "I mean, buck up."

Okay, so she still had to find a phrase that worked for her and didn't remind her of Darian and didn't sound like it came from a *Leave It to Beaver* episode.

Ellie closed her eyes and kept them closed as she asked, "What was the picture of?"

"You. Naked." There was no way to soften the words. She didn't want to soften the words.

"And who shot the picture?"

"Lori, with her cell phone."

"No one else? Not even the guy who undressed me?"

Now it was time for a little softening. "It wasn't a guy who undressed you, Elle. It was Lori."

Ellie's eyes sprang open. Shock, fear, and confusion were in them. "Lori? Is she . . . did she . . ."

"No, she didn't molest you. She just wanted to humiliate you. And everyone in our family. I should have realized this at the pool party, when we figured out that Gen's assistant is Lori's new stepmom." Jayne held Ellie's hand as she went on to explain about Gen being her normal über-bitch self to her assistant and Lori internalizing this and making Gen's daughters pay for the sins of the mother.

And the sins got compounded when one of the golden girls killed her best friend's sister.

"Are you sure there are no duplicates? Of the picture, I mean?"

"Not according to the police."

"Police?" If Ellie hadn't been in bed, she looked like she might've fainted.

"Mom was the one who found out all this stuff when you were still out of it in your diabetic shock and I had . . . I . . ."

"When you had run away from home. Dad told me."

Jayne made a mental note to tell Ellie later about how much fun it *hadn't* been to be out in the world with less than nine hundred dollars and no plan.

"So anyway, the policy interviewed everyone at Meadow's party to see who had and hadn't seen you naked," Jayne said.

"The girls who'd been smoking outside were the only ones. And the cops are pretty sure Lori only e-mailed it to her own address, which they've erased. They don't think the picture's anywhere else. Lori's not that smart, you know?"

Ellie nodded. And squeezed Jayne's hand hard. "Looks like you were right about me."

"About what?"

"Having to think for me. Make my decisions for me." Ellie closed her eyes, and tears seeped down her cheeks.

"Ellie. You are perfectly capable of making your own decisions. But you have to want to make the right decisions, y'know?"

"The right ones aren't as much fun." Ellie sniffed. "Like that FIT scholarship. I totally blew the deadline."

"You'll find another one. I'll help you." Jayne knew this was the perfect spot to clear things up between them.

To get back to being normal.

"So when you say 'right ones,' do you mean decisions like taking your insulin three times a day?"

Ellie didn't look at her. Her head listed to the side, and she watched her heartbeat on one of the monitors. "I think I was only doing it twice a day. Dad got me in the mornings and at night, and no one was around during the summer to do the lunch one."

"Why didn't you call me?"

"Because you hated it. You were sick of helping me."

Ellie had nailed it on the head. The thing was, Jayne hadn't known she'd been so transparent. "You're right, Elle, I was sick of helping you. But do you know why?"

Ellie shook her head, still avoiding Jayne's eyes.

"I looked down at the phone when you called. When I was in the car, on the day of the accident, I looked down. When I ran that red light, you were calling and I was looking to see who was calling."

"Oh God, Jayne. I'm sorry." Ellie started crying. Ugly, loud sobs.

"But Elle, listen." Jayne swallowed over the lump forming in her throat. "When I ran away from home—crap, doesn't that sound stupid?—but when I was gone, you know what I found out? I was at fault. I mean, I could've ignored that call, right? But no, I had to see who it was, even though the light was yellow and I was going totally fast."

"Yeah?" Ellie's sobs had subsided somewhat. Now she was sniffing and trying to catch her breath again.

"Yeah." Jayne thought about the day. The call. The reason for the call. "Elle, why'd you call me? You never said when I talked to you that day."

"Well, you were kinda in the middle of a broken wrist and a crushed car and what was happening with everyone else."

"But why'd you call?"

Ellie closed her eyes. "To thank you. For getting my biology homework. Because I had for . . . got . . . got . . . ten to say it."

The sobs were back.

But this time, Jayne held her.

And started seeing her sister in a different light.

"And Ellie's okay now?" Larry was wearing an olive-and-khaki Hawaiian shirt today. For him, it was a somber look.

"Yep. She's even joking about how she's glad that her picture was taken now, when her body's in the best shape it will probably ever be in." Jayne was lying down on Larry's leather couch, retelling the events of the last couple of days. She knew it was clichéd to be lying down, but she was tired. School had started yesterday, and she was already bored with the non-honors classes she was taking.

But tomorrow that was going to change. Not because of getting into Harvard. But just so she wouldn't be bored. And so she could start liking school again.

Larry stopped watering and seemed to turn the thought over in his head. "I suppose that's a healthy way of looking at it. Then again, a fourteen-year-old saying such a thing worries me a little."

"Yeah, that's what I told her." Jayne looked at the cover of *National Geographic*. But she didn't open it. "Then again, I'd rather have her issues than my issues any day of the week."

He moved closer, watering the plants at Jayne's feet. "You know those three children of mine I mentioned to you before? The ones who are grown now? Well, two had solid enough grades. One went to Berkeley, the other to NYU. The other one, she was the middle one. She had some problems junior year. Discovered boys, alcohol. Her grades slipped. You know where she's at?"

Jayne threw out her first guess. "An online school?"

The doc chuckled again. "No. She's at Yale."

Jayne watched the water drizzle out of his can. "How'd she manage that?"

"In her personal statement, she talked about why she'd had a bad semester." Larry sat in his green easy chair. His eyes point-blankly looked into hers. Open. Honest. "She talked about how that semester had changed her from a girl only worried about her grades to a girl who accidentally got pregnant."

"God. That must've sucked."

Doc sat back, his hands folded over his stomach. "And it did. Recently, you asked me if I'd ever had a week like yours. That week, when Anya told us about being pregnant . . . That week was one of the worst, if not *the* worst, of my life."

"So she just wrote about getting pregnant and she got in?" Jayne had her doubts. Doc was trying to make her feel better. Getting pregnant wasn't something that would stand out in a good way.

"She wrote about the pregnancy—and the abortion."

Jayne didn't say anything. She didn't know if there was anything to say.

Doc's kid had had an abortion? And it had gotten her into Yale?

He must've seen the disbelief in her eyes. "Anya is a very good writer, first and foremost. And in that essay, she was also pretty terrific at figuring out how past mistakes could figure into future successes."

He leaned back again, his eyes unfocused, like he was looking past Jayne and the room they were in. "I'll never forget the title."

For a second, Jayne didn't think he was going to say anything. She waited quietly, though. She knew this was hard for the doc to say.

"She called it"—he cleared his throat and took another pause—"'The Worst Mistake I Ever Had the Misfortune to Learn From.'"

"Are you taking down your Harvard shrine?"

"It wasn't a shr—" Jayne stopped. There was no use arguing with Ellie. She pulled out another thumbtack. "No, I was just rearranging some things."

"Where's the A-hole Award Board?" Ellie sounded stupefied.

"No need for it." This was easier than she'd thought. She was already as far back as the essay she'd done on acid rain in third grade. "I don't need to see all this every single day. Anyway, I want a place to put my photos. I'm taking that photography class, so I need room for the pictures I'll be taking."

Plus, Gen did not like random holes in her walls.

"What brought on the urge to rearrange stuff?"

"New year, new stuff."

"'Stuff'? And you're the wordsmith in the family?" Ellie pushed away from the door and walked down the hall. "Heaven help us."

Jayne had one more drawer to clear out, then she'd be done.

Done with decluttering her room. And starting to feel in control of her own destiny.

She opened a desk drawer, and a black-and-white grainy picture of Brenda Deavers stared back at her. "Six-Year-Old Brain-Dead/Teen at Fault."

It was time to make a fresh start. In every single dusty, murky corner of her life.

She grabbed the half-inch stack of clippings and shoved them into a shoebox decoupaged with roses. She took the box and her chair to the closet, stepped on the chair, and put the box on the top shelf.

In plain sight. But out of constant sight, too.

She was almost ready to call it a night when she saw the cream-colored envelope sticking out of the Arizona history book she'd put it in. It was made out to Donna Deavers in Jayne's all-cap handwriting.

She picked up the envelope, checking the back flap. Yep, it was securely fastened. All she had to do was mail it.

She stared at it. After a while, the letters started blending all together in a swirl of black ink. What was keeping her from mailing it?

Jayne knew the answer. The letter was supposed to make her feel better. But it hadn't. It still didn't. It sure didn't stop that little girl from being dead.

Like Maria had said, contacting Mrs. Deavers wouldn't do anything for anyone other than Jayne.

Before she could think about it anymore, she ripped the letter in two, four, six, eight pieces.

Then she went to her mom's office, adjacent to the exercise room. It was dark. Her parents were at some social event, as usual.

She put the pieces into the shredder, her hand underneath to catch the pieces.

She went back to her room, climbed onto the chair again, and put the pieces into the box on the topmost shelf.

43

SO HOW'D IT GO WITH THE FOLKS?"

Jayne worked on cropping another quarter inch from the photo, not wanting to answer Ryan's question until she'd finished running the sharp blade across the paper. The man's bottom hand was throwing off the proportions of the picture. Other than that, this picture was near perfect—the way it was taken, how it was developed. It was her only one with these specific blacks, whites, and grays, and she'd be really pissed if she screwed it up.

"We're good." Jayne eyeballed the picture. It would do. "We're not perfect. We have too much baggage for that kind of Disney ending." She picked up the picture, her hands cradling it from underneath so she wouldn't leave any prints. "But at least Mom only spent ten minutes trying to change my mind when I told her I wasn't taking all honors classes."

"Only?"

"This was the woman who once spent two hours with me saying I should take seven honors classes rather than six."

"Got it."

They were both in Ryan's bedroom. Another surprise. The walls were light green, and there was a *Wizard of Oz* mural on one wall. All of the knickknacks covering Ryan's shelves were either memorabilia from that movie or textbooks.

Which wasn't surprising—Ryan, Jayne had found out, was valedictorian of her class at Cactus West High.

It'd been only two weeks since that weekend Jayne had crashed on Maria's cot, but it already felt like Ryan was an old friend. They both did honors classes and had an insane love of photography.

"What do you think? A black mat or a white one?"

"Trust your gut." Ryan looked out her window. "You know something? We better do the spray adhesive downstairs. That stuff can asphyxiate us in here."

Jayne was busy studying her picture and wasn't noticing how intently Ryan was looking out the window. "We're not going to interrupt your mom's party, are we?"

"They're just jocks Mom trains in the spring. They're playing with water guns and eating too many Cheez Doodles. They can survive two girls spraying some photographs."

Jayne picked up the things she'd need. "Lead the way."

One their way down, Ryan threw over her shoulder, "By the way, Maria told Darian that she didn't need him at Outreach anymore."

"Really?" Jayne thought about that for a second. It'd be nice to have Darian totally out of her life, that was for sure. Even though they worked at different times now, she still got nervous whenever she saw someone from a distance who looked like him. "Did she tell Meadow that, too?"

"No, she has about ten more hours left of her community service. But they'll be done soon enough."

On the bottom step, Jayne dropped her mats.

"I've got it."

Jayne's skin prickled at the sound of that voice. "Tom?"

"Hey." He looked taller. And tanner. And goofy, like usual.

In a good way. A very good way.

And he didn't seem surprised to see her.

"Ryan." Jayne's voice was more threat than question.

"Well, look at that." Ryan grabbed everything from Jayne's hands. "You two know each other."

"Don't play dumb. We know you're not dumb."

"Well, since we've got that straightened out, you two go catch up. I'll put these in the garage."

Halfheartedly, Jayne said, "The exhibit's tomorrow, though . . ."

"And we both have more than enough time to finish these photos before we turn them in, don't we?" Ryan said smoothly.

Before Jayne could take a breath to say anything else, Ryan had disappeared.

"What exhibit are you showing at?"

Jayne turned back to Tom. They were standing only half a foot apart, but the chasm between them . . . it seemed like it stretched for a mile.

"At All the Sweet Tomorrows? You know that wall they have for all the locals' art? Ryan and I got the owner to put a couple of our things up." She felt like the temperature was rising a good thirty degrees. "You want to see the pictures?"

She started toward the garage, not even waiting for a yes or no. She didn't even think to. She was single-mindedly intent on getting back to Ryan.

Safety in numbers.

The light was on in the garage, and the pictures were propped up, but no Ryan.

"Is this one yours?" Tom was bent over the one Jayne had just been cropping a few minutes ago. Back when she'd been blissfully unaware Tom was under the same roof she was. Back when she was still able to think clearly.

"Yeah." She moved next to him, wildly aware of how close their elbows were to touching. "How could you tell?"

"It's your style." He pointed at the man in the center of the frame, asleep riding the bus, the name "Jose" on a patch over the shirt pocket. A pair of reading glasses was propped on the tip of his nose, a paperback open on his chest. "The irony of this guy riding the bus, probably a mechanic based on the shirt and the grease under his fingernails, reading a romance novel. It's amazing."

"Thanks." Her voice came out quiet and squeaky. Ryan had told her the same thing. Same with Mr. Carlson, her photography teacher, a guy who'd shot some pretty huge print campaigns in his life.

But these words now, from Tom, meant the most. She turned toward him, intent on telling him that.

He was already looking at her.

"Tom, I'm sorry . . ."

He put a hand on her arm, his thumb gently rubbing her skin. "No, I am. I didn't know how much Lori was bullying you. She was always asking me how you were doing, so I thought you were off her radar. Then Ellie told me a couple of weeks ago all the crap she's pulled, and I've been trying to dodge the girl ever since." He looked down and then up again, his eyes bright. "You know nothing ever happened, right?"

Jayne nodded. She knew.

Somehow, their bodies were pressed together. His body was strong and warm against hers. He smelled like Bengay.

"Can I make it up to you?" The words were a whisper.

"How?" Another whisper.

"I was thinking"—his Adam's apple bobbed up and down— "that being your devoted boyfriend would be a great place to start?"

She leaned in. He leaned in.

The kiss was warm and gentle.

And the best one of her life.

44

HEY, LOVEBIRDS. Mom and Dad are home." Ellie came into the family room and turned on the TV.

Jayne pulled away from Tom. She smiled, noticing the flush on Tom's cheeks. She wondered if she had the same rosy cheeks.

She looked at the clock over the TV. They'd been kissing for about an hour. Not their record, but definitely a high scorer.

"What are you watching?" Gen came in, a pile of mail in hand, flipping through it. "Is that a shark eating another shark?"

"Research. For a paper." Ellie put up the volume with the remote.

Gen grabbed the remote from her and turned down the volume. "I'm glad everyone's here. Remember that dog trainer story I worked on a couple of months ago?"

Tom squeezed Jayne's hand. She'd told him about Gen wanting her to be on her show during sweeps and having to settle for the dog trainer instead.

"Well, my producer—Cameron—sent that tape to one of the cable news stations." She held her breath before blurting out,

"And I got a call today to do a once-a-month slice-of-life segment about Phoenix."

"And . . ." Sean Thompkins came in just then, grabbing his wife's shoulders from behind. "Tell them the rest."

"Well, the segment's only five minutes, so how much can you really do in five minutes . . ."

"Not that. The other thing."

Gen looked at him, confusion on her face. He rolled his eyes and pulled a letter out of the pile she had. "This. Tell them about this."

"Oh. That's right." She pulled out a letter from the envelope. Jayne saw the green palm in the upper-left-hand corner. She clutched Tom's hand between both of hers. "It says, 'Dear Parents of Jayne Thompkins: We are pleased to announce that your daughter has won Senior Student for the class of 2007 . . .'"

Gen looked up. "Nice work, Jayne. I knew you'd do it." She looked at her watch. "If you'll excuse me, everyone, I have to call Atlanta before their segment producer leaves for the day."

And with that statement, she left.

Jayne was still in shock. Not about her mom. She was used to her. But the award. She'd totally forgotten about having applied for it.

"Wow. Mom really is self-centered, isn't she?" Ellie shook her head before bouncing off the couch and crashing into Jayne. "Congratulations! I guess this means no Jayne at summer vacation." In a whisper, she added, "Lucky dog."

"Yeah, kid, nice work." Her dad waited his turn and then enveloped her in a big bear hug. "What do you want to celebrate? Pizza, dinner out, a movie?"

"Sugar-free cake!" Ellie and Jayne said it in unison.

"Cake it is, then." He kissed Jayne's forehead. "I'm very proud of you. Remember that, okay?"

She nodded and started to tear up when she saw him tear up.

"Get out of here, Dad. Go on, before we all just fall into a huge, teary mess."

He left to go to All the Sweet Tomorrows a few minutes later. Ellie turned up the volume and switched on the Style Network.

"I knew that if anyone got the Senior Student award, it would be you." Tom whispered this in her ear.

"Honestly, I forgot about it. So much crap happened and it kind of fell to the wayside." In a whisper, she added, "Plus, I didn't think I deserved it anymore."

He held her hand tightly. "You deserve it, Jayne. You're an amazing girl, you know that?"

"Not really." She pressed her lips to his cheek. Her mouth turned up into a smile. "But then again, you're a pretty smart guy, Mr. Valedictorian, so you'd know."

45

Jayne."

Jayne looked up from the computer. Maria had her looking up stats to put into a grant proposal to ask for more money for Outreach. Then she could get more phones. Another person to run things when she was out of town.

And a new door for the back that locked.

"Are you ready for your test run?"

"Test run?" Jayne's voice squeaked out. "I don't think I'm ready for that. Isn't there a test I should take first? An essay to write, maybe?"

Jayne was grasping. She felt it. Maria probably could hear it in her excuses.

"No test, no essay. Just some phone time, with me on the other end monitoring the call and stepping in when I need to." She put a hand on her shoulder. "You'll do great, Jayne. I can feel it."

Jayne nodded mutely. The only thing she felt was sick.

"Wh—when do you want to do the test run?" Fear had made Jayne's mouth go dry and her mind blank.

"Next call." Maria tilted her head toward her office. "I have two phones in there. Ryan will patch the next call through to me."

Ten minutes later, when the phone finally rang, Jayne's heart about jumped out of her chest. She wasn't ready for this. Was Maria a crazy nut job?

Maria answered the phone on her desk. "Who do we have today, Ryan?"

She nodded while getting the information. Jayne wiped her palms on her jeans. She sat at the conference table adjacent to Maria, a tan rotary-dial phone in front of her.

Maria covered the mouthpiece. "It's a girl named Tammy. Write it down so you remember it." Jayne did as instructed. "It makes the person feel more secure talking to you if you call them by their name and not something else or nothing at all because you forgot. Of course, it's probably going to be a fake name.

"Our girl Tammy is contemplating having sex with her boyfriend for the first time. We are here to listen to her make her own decision. Nothing else. Got it?"

Jayne nodded. She was weak with relief. It wasn't a suicide call. *Thank you, God.*

"You ready?"

Jayne nodded.

"Are you able to talk, Jayne? This call is yours. I'll just be listening in."

Jayne caught herself in the middle of yet another nod. "Um, yes. Yes, I am ready."

"Good. Now pick up the phone." Maria uncovered the mouth of her phone. "Put her through, Ryan."

"This is Jayne at Arizona Outreach. Is this Tammy?" At least

Jayne had read enough of the manual to figure out how to start the conversation. Based on Maria's approving nod, she'd gotten it right.

"Yeah. I mean, yes." The girl sounded like she was twelve.

"How old are you, Tammy?" Jayne couldn't go on without knowing her age for sure.

"I'm sixteen. I'll be seventeen next month."

"And what do you want to talk about today?"

"I ... I've been thinking about having sex." After a brief pause, she added, "With my boyfriend. Just so you know, I'm not about to have sex with a random guy or anything."

Tammy laughed, a little too loud and fake. She was nervous. Jayne decided to take some cues from Larry to get to the meat of this conversation. "And how do you feel about that, Tammy?"

"I—I guess I'm ready."

This Tammy *chica* was sounding a lot like Ellie. Unsure, wishy-washy. In need of guidance. Jayne felt something stir in her, the same something that had given her the energy to pull unsuspecting guys off her sister.

"You guess?"

"Well, I mean, does anyone know for sure?"

Jayne didn't even know if Maria was okay with what she was saying or not. She didn't even think to look at her. "For something as important as sex, I think you need to be sure."

"But how do you know?" Tammy's voice was soft, and it sounded a lot like she was near tears.

Jayne twiddled the phone cord between her fingers. How did a person know? She went with her honest opinion. "I think you know when you can look into your boyfriend's eyes and know he's your best friend. And that he'd be the last person in the world to hurt you."

The line was silent. Jayne looked up at Maria. She gave her the thumbs-up sign.

Tammy's voice asked, "What if you really, really like the guy, though?"

"I think that at one time or another, we all really, really like something. Like me, I really, really like ice cream. But if I give in to it, I'll get really sick. Ice cream is not my friend."

Tammy didn't say anything. Jayne counted ten Mississippis, and then she pulled a Larry: "Tammy, what are you feeling right now?"

"Like maybe I can't honestly say I can trust him."

Jayne quietly exhaled her breath. She hadn't even known she'd been holding it. "And do you want your first time to be with a guy who might be with someone else tomorrow? Or has an STD he hasn't told you about?"

"No." The answer was barely audible.

Silence came over the line once more. Jayne mouthed to Maria, "Now what?" Maria mouthed back, "Just stay on."

A minute of silence followed. Jayne was keeping track with her watch.

"I still don't know." The girl on the other side let out her own breath. "Can't you just tell me whether I should or shouldn't?"

Jayne caught Maria shaking her head at her. "I can't, Tammy. All you can do is trust your gut."

There was a muffled sound in the background. "I've gotta go now. Thanks. Bye."

"Tammy . . ." But she'd already hung up.

Jayne dropped the phone back on its hook, disgusted. "That was hugely unsatisfying."

"That's how most of the calls go, though." Maria hung up her own phone and came over to Jayne. "All you can do is guide them, not tell them what to do. You know, that whole teach-a-man-to-fish philosophy."

Maria squatted in front of her. "By the way, nice job. Especially for your first time out."

"I know I screwed up . . ."

Maria waved a hand. "You're always a lot harder on yourself than anyone else is. Do you know that?"

"Tom told me that. Ellie, too."

"See?"

Jayne swallowed. It was time to come clean. She respected Maria too much not to. "I didn't finish the manual."

Maria smiled. "None of us do. We all think the manual's a waste of time. Until we're thrown into our first call. Then we all seem to speed-read the sucker."

Jayne smiled. Maria did likewise.

"I guess I'll go do that."

"Sounds good." Maria got up. "By the way, I never told you. I love the hair. It suits you."